The Pet Nanny 2:
Libby Goes To A New School

The Pet Nanny 2: Libby Goes To A New School
Copyright © 2024 by Leisa Braband

Published in the United States of America

Library of Congress Control Number: 2024926911
ISBN   Paperback: 979-8-89091-794-2
ISBN   Hardback: 979-8-89091-795-9
ISBN   eBook: 979-8-89091-796-6

All rights reserved. No part of this publication may be reproduced, stored in a retrieval system or transmitted in any way by any means, electronic, mechanical, photocopy, recording or otherwise without the prior permission of the author except as provided by USA copyright law.

The opinions expressed by the author are not necessarily those of ReadersMagnet, LLC.

ReadersMagnet, LLC
10620 Treena Street, Suite 230 | San Diego, California, 92131 USA
1.619. 354. 2643 | www.readersmagnet.com

Book design copyright © 2024 by ReadersMagnet, LLC. All rights reserved.

Cover design by Ericka Obando
Interior design by Don De Guzman

The Pet Nanny 2: Libby Goes To A New School

LEISA BRABAND

CHAPTER 1

End Of Summer

It seemed lately all I could do was daydream, and at times when I had scary thoughts, I'd day-nightmare. Like just now I stretched out on my bed not wanting to get up and face the day. I was thinking back at how much had happened in just the past three months, and how much had changed. But worst of all, I started panicking thinking of how much my life would change even more in the next few weeks.

Three months ago, my parents decided to get a divorce. That meant my mom and I moved to downtown Chicago, far away from where we had lived in Palos Heights, a suburb in Chicago, with my father. I wasn't happy at all leaving my friends and living in a one room apartment with my mother.

But all that changed when I got a job, a paying job! I became the building's official pet nanny and all summer I took care of five cats, four dogs, and one guinea pig. Even though I am only twelve years old, I run my own pet sitting business, with a little help from my mother. Okay, maybe more than a little bit of help from my mother. I fantasize that if I had a pet of my own, life would be perfect.

But then I realize it's late August and one look at my Hello Kitty calendar and my heart starts to race. School would begin soon, and I would be going to a new school. I wouldn't know any of the other kids or the teachers. I would be going into eighth grade and most probably everyone would know each other. I would be the "new kid". No one wants to be the new kid.

But my biggest fear was how I would go back to school and still be able to care for the animals that depended on me. Until I knew my school schedule, I could put that worry on the back burner. I would do it somehow. Maybe George, the building engineer, would have some ideas. After all, he was the one who introduced me to neighbors who needed someone to take care of their fur babies. George seemed to know everything. If anyone could help, it would be George.

I shifted to my side and had another worrisome train of thought. Tomorrow I would be celebrating my thirteenth birthday. I was going to be a teenager! Maybe "celebrating" wasn't the right word because at this moment, my parents had not mentioned my birthday once. What if they forgot? If I was honest, they never forgot before, but now everything was different. After being separated most of the summer, my parents reunited. In fact, we all live together in a new apartment in the same building where I am the pet nanny. My parents no longer fight like they did when they were going to divorce. It's almost worse – now they kiss and cuddle *a lot*.

There was a knock on my bedroom door. My mother looked at me and sighed. "Libby, what is wrong with you?"

I didn't answer.

"Earth to Libby. Earth to Libby. Come in, Libby." I gave her a scowl and a disgruntled "What?"

"I'm trying to talk to you, Libby. Cat got your tongue?" Ever since I started watching dogs and cats my mother liked to talk in animal metaphors.

"Nothing is wrong Mom. I just don't feel like talking. I'm fine," I finally responded even though I was anything but fine. I started going over my list of fears again until my mother shouted.

"Libby!" My mom tried to get my attention.

"You better leave now to check on Charley and Felix. You're already late and you know those cats can tell time."

I realized this was just a reprieve and my mom would continue questioning me when I got back from taking care of my cat charges. But for now I looked forward to some cat caresses.

CHAPTER 2

Einstein, the Cat Confidante

My mom was right. Felix, a gray tiger-striped cat, and Charley, a wanna-be lion groomed to look like the king of the jungle, were waiting right inside their door for me. More accurately, they were waiting for their food and water bowls to be replenished. I pushed my way in, careful that neither cat escaped, and quickly attended to their meal. Their owner, Kelly, was a stewardess, so both cats were used to being left alone for long periods of time. They had a new litter box that was automatic, and I was grateful because it meant once they were distracted by food, I could escape.

After visiting Felix and Charley, I stopped to visit my favorite cat, Einstein. I know it is wrong to have favorites, but I can't help myself. Einstein is about as close to a human as you can get. I swear he understands everything I say, and because I believe that I talk to him constantly.

"Einstein! Einstein! Libby is here! Where are you, Einstein?"

Einstein is usually waiting inside the door when I come to take care of him, but I was a little earlier than usual today. He was probably still snoozing. I couldn't wait to talk with him and share my woes with him. He is such a good listener. I loved to put him over my shoulder and stroke his back while he nuzzled my neck and periodically made soft mew sounds indicating he was listening.

Prompted by the sounds of his cat food can being opened, Einstein, a slick Siamese cat, appeared out of nowhere. He reminded me of George who would also appear the moment you needed him in

the building hallways or at your front door, and then disappear when you didn't need him. Einstein waited patiently for his food and water bowls to be placed on the floor. While he ate, I dealt with his litter box. Not my favorite job, but a necessity for cat hygiene.

Finally, Einstein and I settled down for our chat at the kitchen island. He jumped up to be on eye level with me while I sat on the kitchen stool, and narrowly missed the Yeti mug that his mother, Mimi, left behind yesterday when she ran out to catch her overnight flight for work. She would be back this afternoon, but in the meantime, Einstein was all mine.

"Einstein, you are so lucky you are a cat. You don't even know when your birthday is, or if you did, you wouldn't care. But I'm not a cat, and I do care about my birthday. Tomorrow is my birthday – August 30 – and I am pretty sure my parents forgot. I can't believe there will be no celebration. No cake, no balloons, no presents, no party. And worst of all, Einstein, your mom will be back, and I can't even come over here to get kitty kisses."

Einstein gently purred in agreement, and I noticed he fell asleep at some point during my litany of complaints. I placed him on the couch in the sun streaming from the single window overhead and went back home to check for clues that my parents perhaps did remember my birthday.

Back at home I checked the official calendar hung in the kitchen cabinet. There was a blue star on August 30th but no notes indicating that plans were in the process. My parents were both at work so I could feel free to search closets and under the bed for presents. I checked the desk drawers for birthday cards but there were none. It looked like they did forget my birthday.

My biggest wish for my birthday was to receive a dog or cat of my very own. I loved watching other people's pets, but so wanted to be a pet mommy, not just a pet nanny. When my dad moved back in with us in a larger apartment, I thought maybe my parents would reconsider and grant my wish. But there was no evidence in the apartment that I would be receiving a pet, so I concentrated on hoping that they simply remembered my birthday.

I went to check my phone to see if there were any messages from my folks of when to expect them home for lunch. Oops! I left the phone at Einstein's house. I grabbed my Libby keys and ran down the hall to the other side of the building. As I reached a bend in the hallway I heard voices from the other end. Einstein's apartment was hidden from view from where I was but I distinctly heard two voices: George's and Einstein's mother Mimi's.

"Don't you think Libby is a little whacky George?" Mimi was saying.

"Whacky?" George questioned Mimi. "In what way?"

Oh, my, they are talking about me, I thought.

"Well, she talks to my cat. All the time. About her personal problems and worries and hopes and dreams. Doesn't she have a human to talk to?" Mimi was complaining about *her* talking to Einstein. But how did she know?

"How do you know she talks to Einstein?" George asked. I could just picture his one eyebrow raised as he challenged Mimi.

"I'll tell you how," Mimi said with pride in her voice. "I installed a "pet cam". It's like a nanny cam and it records everything while I am gone. I time it for when I think Libby will be sitting with Einstein."

"I don't know this for a fact," George uttered in a warning voice, "But I think such devices are illegal. They violate people's rights to privacy. I hope for your sake Libby never finds out you violated her rights. Her mom works for lawyers, you know. Plus, you'll lose yourself the best pet sitter you ever had."

I couldn't wait any longer. I had to get my phone. So I rounded the corner and as cheerily as I could I said, "Hi Mimi. Hi George. I forgot my phone this morning in your apartment. May I go get it?" I swallowed the comments I wanted to make about her pet cam since I didn't want to lose my job watching Einstein.

"I'll get it for you, Libby. I wouldn't want you and Einstein to get caught up in a long conversation." Mimi turned and went into her apartment.

George looked uncertain of what to say so instead he patted me on the shoulder and said, "Hey, it's your birthday eve! Do you have a special birthday outfit picked out?"

I looked at George shocked that he knew tomorrow was my birthday. George seemed to know everything about everybody! I blinked and in typical George fashion, he had disappeared, and Mimi reappeared with my phone. I muttered a thank you and went back to my apartment wondering why George thought I should have a special birthday outfit. I hope that he knows something I don't! Maybe my parents didn't forget! Distracted by this thought I hurried home to look through my closet for my birthday outfit (just in case!)

CHAPTER 3

Libby's Birthday

The bedroom was suddenly bathed in light. I tried opening my tear-crusted eyes to see what was going on but at the same time I struggled to keep dreaming. It was such a nice dream… what was it again? Oh, yes, it was my *birthday*, and I got a dog from my parents. It was a creamy brown small dog, but not too small, and not too big. It was like Goldilocks – JUST RIGHT! And its bark was not like other dogs' barks. It wasn't loud or piercing. It was soft like a song. And its smell was sweet, not like other dogs who smelled like a combination of dog food and mud breath. And it TALKED! Like in English. It was saying, "Libby! Libby! Wake up, Libby!"

Whaaat? What was going on? The last thing I remembered was last night. I finally fell asleep after crying myself to sleep. I was worried that my parents had forgotten my birthday the next day. In fact, I was sure of it. They hadn't said a thing, and my searching the apartment high and low did not turn up any clues to the contrary. And evidently, the day had dawned and today was August 30th – the morning of my thirteenth birthday. And when I finally opened my eyes to see if the dog I dreamed about was fur real (get it? *Fur real?)*, instead of a new furry friend staring at me in the face, it was my mother.

"Get up, sleepy head. Time to celebrate the most important day of the year!" My mother was practically wagging in anticipation. *Oh no, she was the dog in my dream. Well, it figures. Her creamy brown morning hair was a little dog-like.*

Wait a minute. Did she say "most important day of the year?" Was it a trick? Was August 30th something else other than my birthday? So I tested her.

"OK, Mom. I'll bite. What is today?"

"Your birthday, silly! Now, get up. Your Dad is waiting in the kitchen and if you don't get in there right away, he just might burn down the house." My mom talks in riddles sometimes. What was she talking about anyway?

I slowly walked down the short hallway to the kitchen and saw a mysterious glow from the kitchen table. My mother scooted past me and took her position next to my dad who was holding a bowl of melting ice cream with a lit candle in the middle. And not just any ice cream, but butter pecan with fudge topping, whip cream and encircled with maraschino cherries. Not just one cherry, but at least a dozen. No.... not a dozen, THIRTEEN! They did remember. And as my parents finished singing "Happy Birthday, Libby", I shut my eyes and blew out the candle. I wished that my parents bought me a dog for my birthday. But no worries, they had all day to make my dream come true.

After the best breakfast ever of an ice cream sundae my mother insisted that I shower and dress in whatever new outfit a big gift-wrapped box contained. It ended up being a bedazzled t-shirt with "THE PET NANNY" printed on the front. Underneath the words was a printed picture of Rocky, my favorite dog charge. Rocky was an American Eskimo and we pet-sat him in our apartment every few weeks for a week at a time when his parents traveled. I couldn't wait until the next time we pet-sat Rocky.

Well, here I was all dressed up and no where to go! That's a favorite phrase of my mom. I never really understood it until now. What was the use of wearing new clothes if no one was there to appreciate them? And just like that, the doorbell rang. It was George, my favorite building engineer (my only building engineer).

"What's up, George?" My eyes focused on the wrapped gift in George's hands. Could it be for me? He did mention my birthday yesterday. Of course it was for me!

"Happy birthday, Libby. I have a little something for you," he said as he pushed the small, wrapped box into my hands.

I first checked it for airholes. Better than anyone else George knew how much I wanted a dog. Or a cat. But this box was too small for either a dog or a cat. But not too small for a turtle. I never had a turtle. But don't turtles need water? I better rip off the wrapping before it died.

"Oh no you don't, Libby." My mother took the box from my eager hands. I looked at her in alarm. She took my gift from George away. That's just not right, and I was about to tell her so, when she said, "What is the first thing you do when someone gives you a present?

I was quick to answer before the turtle died. "Open the card?"

But there was no card. George looked embarrassed, but as usual saved the day by saying he was a "living card" and was there to recite what a card would, only in person.

"Good try you two but not the answer. What do you always do when someone does something nice for you?" My mother repeated her original question.

It came to me in a flash. "Thank you, George for remembering my birthday and giving me a present. May I open it now, before the turtle dies?" I asked posed to tear the package open and give the turtle mouth to mouth before it died.

"Please do, but just a hint. It's not a turtle."

"Oh, no. Not a turtle? It must be a goldfish then! And how much water could be in there? It has to be dead!"

But the box didn't contain a potential pet. It was a simple key. To what I wondered?

"Libby's mother, can I take Libby to her birthday gift? We can be back in a half hour."

"Sure, George," my mother replied right away. It seemed like my mom was in on the big secret because she didn't question George any further. I wondered where we were going and what my gift was that could be opened by a key and as I followed George, we quickly arrived at the stairwell leading to the storage units.

George put the security code in the outer door and showed me how to use the code, which he whispered. "1,2,3,4".

"That's it? That's not very secure, George. It's the first thing anyone would try," I pointed out.

"Really? Well, it's a good thing then that each storage unit has its own key so if they do break the code on the outer door, they still won't be able to get into the individual units." I nodded at his wisdom, wondering what my key would lead to.

"Here we are," George stated as I stared at a floor-to-ceiling wooden slatted square unit at the back of the room of similar storage units.

"Happy Birthday," George said as he put out his hand for the key.

"Always say ABACADABRA before opening the door to Libby's Clubhouse, or the magic inside could escape!" And before I could puzzle what he meant he opened the door. It was magical. Bright pink drapes hung from the top of the unit to the bottom for privacy. There was a big stuffed chair and floor lamp next to it, perfect for reading. And a table next to it on the other side perfect for placing a soda and a snack while I read. On the floor was a wall-to-wall shaggy white rug, as soft as Rocky's fur. And what was that in the corner? A mini-fridge! And a bookshelf with books. I scanned the titles and realized I never read any of them. And what was that? A treasure chest?

"George, is that a Pirate's treasure chest?" I asked already wondering what it could contain.

"Close," George said, "But no cigar." My mother would say that same phrase and it didn't make any more sense when George said it.

"What is it then, George?" I asked already opening the lid.

"That is a hope chest. Young ladies used to get them when they were about your age to prepare for when they got married. Friends and family would help them get ready by giving them gifts for the house they would eventually have with their husband. I put something in yours that you can use first in your clubhouse."

I unfolded a beautiful patchwork quilt of fabric squares. Each square was either plain pink or a square with a Hello Kitty picture. It was beautiful.

"It can get cold down here in the basement. I thought you could use a blanket to keep warm in the winter. Well come on, I promised to have you back upstairs right about now." George pointed to something on the wall. It was a clock! But not just any clock – it was a rhinestone kitty kat with a clock-face on its tummy and a tail suspended from the bottom that clicked as it went back and forth like the metronome that was on top of my piano back home.

"Thank you, George. I love it. I love all of it. It's perfect. I miss my treehouse so much from my house in Palos Heights. How did you know?

"I don't know, Libby. But you might have mentioned that a thousand times." George smiled as we returned to my apartment on the first floor. As I opened the door to the apartment, I turned to thank George once again for my Clubhouse, but he had disappeared. And I didn't even say Abacadabra. Oh, well, I would catch up with him later. I turned back to the door, but the apartment was dark. Did my parents go somewhere without me? Well, that was rude. And on my birthday!

But before I could contemplate where they might have gone, the lights mysteriously turned on and I noticed a dozen faces shouting "SURPRISE! HAPPY BIRTHDAY"! And one shaggy face ran up on all fours barking his own version of "happy birthday". It was Rocky, my favorite dog charge, and his parents, Kara and Carl. In the corner were my friends from Palos Heights, and my Aunt Lori, my favorite aunt and realtor (my only aunt and realtor) and, of course, my parents. And George! Wait a minute, he was just with me outside the door. How did he get inside with the rest of the crowd? It's amazing how he reappears as quickly as he disappears. Just one more surprise on top of my surprise party. This birthday keeps getting better and better.

My mom had everyone grab a dish and help themselves to the Chinese lunch buffet set up on the kitchen counter. The furniture in the living room had been moved so that a long portable table and chairs were available for everyone to sit and eat. Each place setting had a fortune cookie and a wrapped party favor.

"Can we open our gifts?" my friend Brenda asked my mom. I was thinking the same thing but was afraid my mom would reprimand me for being impolite. Brenda seemed to think it was worth the risk.

"Let me explain first, please. Everyone has a party favor that is a lucky charm. Since this is Libby's 13th birthday, I thought she and her birthday guests should be surrounded with a little extra luck. Since Brenda prompted me, I'll ask that she open first and then ask that each of you do the same and show us what you got! Brenda – go for it!"

Brenda opened her gift so quickly that the purple rabbit's foot flew across the table and hit Aunt Lori in the head. The luck started already that it didn't hit Aunt Lori in the eye! The others oohed and aahed as they opened their gifts. There was a metal horseshoe (thank Goodness that didn't fly across the table!), a lucky penny, a four-leaf clover, a lucky star. Thirteen gifts in total – my mom thought of everything!

At the end of lunch my mom and dad came out of the kitchen carrying a multi-tiered birthday cake decorated on top with an edible rainbow. No pot of gold underneath it, I noticed, or a dog or cat, but the new I-pad they gave me was a great gift. And a timely one as school started next week.

Ugggh. School. Having my old school chums visit today was just another reminder of how much I missed them and my old school and how scared I was to start at a new school and hopefully make new friends. I would need all the lucky charms I could get!

CHAPTER 4

SCHOOL ORIENTATION

"Libby, Libby, wake up! WAKE UP!" My mom was practically screaming at me. This waking me up thing was getting old.

"Whaaat?" I said through half open eyes and in a grumpier than usual voice. I am not what people call "a morning person".

"I took out a few things for you to try on. See what looks the best and come out to the living room right away. We're going to school!" my mom directed.

OK, now I know she lost it. It was Sunday on Labor Day weekend. One of my last days of peace before I had to face a new school.

"Mom, I know you know today is Sunday. What gives?" I tried to be kind. After all, Mom was getting older. She was at least thirty. I heard people lose their memory when they get old.

I finally opened my eyes all the way and looked at my mom. She looked frantic and something else….. She looked guilty!

"You see," she began, "I was so busy getting ready for your birthday I ignored a lot of other unrelated emails, and one of them, well actually several of them, were from your new school. Today is a mandatory orientation session at the school." She looked at her watch, and said, "In 30 minutes. Thankfully the school is only ten minutes away. PLEASE Libby, get up and get dressed. NOW."

She left me no time to argue or wonder what I would find in 30 minutes. Would it be a school like what I was used to? Would it be smaller, bigger, or just right? What is "just right"? I was about to start

counting my expectations when mom's voice pierced the bedroom door. "I mean NOW Libby Lancaster."

I brushed my teeth and washed my face. I looked at the assortment of clothes mom took out for me. The jeans and tie-dyed shirt looked good, except when I pulled on the jeans, they were short. By a couple of inches. "MOM!!!!" I screamed.

She came barreling into the bedroom and saw the problem right away. "Oh, no. All summer you wore shorts and a t-shirt. I had no idea you had grown so much. Okay, well take that off and put on your Sunday dress." But when I did, it was also shorter, but my mom decided while the length was not ideal, it looked less tacky than "flood jeans" as she called my too short jeans.

A few minutes later we left my dad to take care of the morning pets and we took an Uber to my new school. As we pulled up, I was surprised by how colorful it was, and how many windows there were. My mom had explained previously it was a private school that had grades Kindergarten through eighth grade. That was about all she explained, so as we left the Uber, I was slow to follow her into the school. I was still taking it all in. It was several stories high and each floor on the outside of the building was another colored stripe. The playground equipment in the yard out front was a different color scheme, and even though I was too old for such things, it still held an appeal for my inner jungle gymnast. And then there was all the doors on the outside – they were different colors too. I wondered if there was a code to the colors, and hoped to get the answer inside, where my mom led the way. I casually noticed the sign in front which read: EDISON ELEMENTARY.

Mom was consulting an email I assumed she received from the school when she said, "Ah hah! Here's the room!" She knocked and a female voice said, "Come in!"

She was so young. I thought we were going to meet my teacher. And she had on an identical top to the tie-dyed top I was going to wear with my jeans! We could have been twins if I didn't grow so much!

"How do you do," my mother was saying. I am Mrs. Lancaster – Libby's mother. I hope we are not late."

"Actually, you are not. You are right on time. I like punctuality. You get an A!" The woman beamed at my mother in approval before turning to look at me. Oh, no, she spotted my short skirt.

"You must be Libby. I am your 8th grade teacher, Ms. Hart. Let me guess. You haven't worn that dress all summer, have you?" she asked me.

"I haven't – but how did you know?" I asked my new teacher.

"I remember when I turned 13. Everything changed – including my height. But don't worry, you'll be joining 19 other students with similar problems. We'll get through the next year together. And as far as clothes fitting, we wear uniforms here so your clothes will be JUST RIGHT!" Aaaahhh, she used the Goldilocks principle. I think I was going to like her.

In the next few minutes, Ms. Hart explained that she believed in non-traditional learning. While she would teach the state required subjects like Math, Science and English, she would also teach other subjects that she hoped would inspire her students to consider their future careers. She was telling my mother that it was never too early or late to decide what path your life would take. On Fridays, Ms. Hart explained, we will switch places. The students will teach, and I and the other students will learn. A week before, I will have a topic board set up at the front of the room, and each student will have a chance to pick their topic that they want to research and teach the following Friday. Ms. Hart noted, "this Friday you will get to pick your first topic."

Ms. Hart continued. "For Wednesday, the first day of school, I want you to fill out this Questionnaire before class." She handed me a sheet of paper with the following statements and corresponding blank spaces to fill in:

My Name is:_____
Three Words I would use to describe myself:_____
My age and birthday:_____
Three Things I love to do:_____
My favorite color is:_____
My favorite wild animal:_____
My favorite song:_____

"These questions should help the class get to know you from the start." Ms. Hart got up and showed us to the door.

She turned to face us, pointing to the right. "You'll need to do two more things before you leave school today. Down in room 101, please pick up Libby's uniforms. I should mention that from time to time we have NO UNIFORM DAY and you are welcome to wear pretty much anything you want. Even tie- dyed shirts like I have on."

She looked at me expectantly and I said, "How did you know I have one just like yours?"

"Doesn't all the cool kids?" she laughed. She had a nice laugh. I hoped to make her laugh more throughout the year. This is a teacher I would not want to disappoint.

"Also," Ms. Hart was continuing, "at the end of the hall is the gymnasium. You'll need to go spin the bingo ball cage to determine what session (a.m. or p.m.) Libby will be attending. Our enrollment was higher than expected this year and we needed to go to split shifts. So if you get an even number Libby will be attending morning sessions from 7:30 a.m. to 12:00 noon. If you get an odd number, she'll be attending afternoon sessions from 1:00 p.m. to 5:30 p.m."

"Oh, my. I had no idea that was the case. You see, both my husband and I work. The morning session would work so much better with our schedules." My mom frowned.

I was thinking it would also work so much better with my pet sitting, but my mother had warned me not to bring up our pet sitting business, so I kept quiet.

"Well, there were several emails that addressed this issue. Perhaps you didn't read them carefully?" Ms. Hart was trying to give mom an out. She was very kind.

"I guess that is the case. So, this is sort of a lotto, then?" my mom asked.

"Exactly! Just think, you have a 50/50 chance of getting an even number. I have a feeling that you will, and if you do, you should buy a lotto ticket on the way home."

We passed Room 101 on the way to the gymnasium and we were pleased to go through the uniform assembly line relatively quickly. First, I stepped behind a curtain to be measured. Then the seamstress measuring me handed me a slip of paper after sizing me up with all my pertinent sizes. I was then directed to a long table where blouses and skirts were lined up and gave my paper listing my sizes to the table attendant. The last station was the collection table where my mother handed over her credit card. Slowly. When she saw the receipt she paled a little bit, but that could have been my imagination. It was a little cold in Room 101.

Moments later we stood in a short line of anxious parents and pupils spinning the bingo ball cage, hoping for even or odd numbers, depending on what best fit their schedule. And even though I will never be a morning person, I really wanted the early session so I could still be the Pet Nanny. The older man in charge (who coincidentally reminded me of George, for no particular reason), said, "Let 'er spin!" I couldn't believe how many times it tumbled before spitting out a single ball. The man handed it to me. And I dropped it. And it rolled under the bleachers before I could see what number was imprinted on the ball.

"Well don't look at me. Go find it. I'm too old for crawling under bleachers," the old man said sounding grumpier than ever.

I ran to the bleachers and slid under them amid spider webs. And even though my hand reached for the ball, I still didn't know the number because it was too dark under the bleachers to see.

"Honey, what is it?" my mom prompted.

"Come on kid. I don't have all day," the man grumbled.

I savored the moment before emerging full of cobwebs holding a small gray kitten with green eyes. "Look at what I found!" I exclaimed. The cat mewed loudly echoing my excitement.

My mom and the old man looked at me with impatience. "But what about the ball?" my mom asked, throwing her arms up in disgust.

"Oh, yeah," I said, as I crawled back underneath to retrieve the ball holding the kitten tight.

CHAPTER 5

Calm Before The Storm

"George, is this for ME?" I asked George as my mom and I returned home from school orientation. We had decided to walk home from school, and remarkably walking my mom was not much different than walking the dogs. Every time she saw something of interest we had to stop and investigate. Just like the dogs I walk!

George acted like he didn't know what I was talking about. But I pointed at the banner above the front door of the building that read, "CONGRATULATIONS LIBBY, THE EARLY BIRD!" George sheepishly 'fessed up.

"I was so happy to hear that you drew an even number and you'll be going to school on the early shift. That means you'll continue being the Pet Nanny. All your furry customers and their parents will be happy as well!", George exclaimed.

"But George, how did you know? It literally just happened!" I was so confused. How long did it take for me and mom to walk home anyway? And how did George find out? Did mom call him and if she did, why would she?

George answered, "Jerry told me. He called me right after you FINALLY fetched the bingo ball from under the bleachers."

I was even more confused. "George, who is Jerry?" And as I asked the question it dawned on me that Jerry was the grumpy old man (who did remind me vaguely of George).

"Jerry is my brother. He works as the vice principal at your new school. I told him to expect you and your mom today and how

important it was that you get the early shift in the upcoming school year. I am so glad that it all worked out. And Jerry was so grateful that you found his cat, even though he was trying to keep the cat on the down low. You're really not supposed to keep pets on the school premises." George acted as if this was not a big deal at all, but to me it was further proof that George (and evidently his brother Jerry) was capable of miraculous things.

Our attention was grabbed by a squeaky voice approaching from the sidewalk. "Libby! Are you just returning home? Did you forget to take care of Einstein this morning?" It was Mimi, Einstein's mother and initiator of the "Pet Cam Dispute".

"Hi, Mimi," I managed to say cordially enough, keeping my dislike in check. "Einstein is fine! I had school orientation this morning, so my dad took care of him."

"Whaaat?" Mimi's face turned bright red, and she seethed with anger. "I hired YOU, Libby Lancaster, not a stranger. I do not allow strangers to go inside my home. And Einstein is probably traumatized by having someone invade his home that he does not know."

"Oh, don't worry about that, Mimi. My dad and my mom have gone with me several times so Einstein is familiar with them both." I didn't think before I spoke. This did not help my case at all because we went from her venting over a single incident to multiple stints of "house invasion."

"You're fired, Libby! You leave me no choice. You violated my trust and the security of my home." Mimi stormed off into the house leaving me, my mom and George speechless.

George spoke first. "Don't worry, Libby. You know Mimi. She'll calm down after she sees Einstein is okay. But in the future, it would probably be wise to tell a pet owner if there is any change in your arrangement to take care of their pet. Thankfully, those times will probably be minimal now that you have the early school schedule."

I hoped George was right, but my confidence was vanishing.

The next day was Labor Day and two days before school started. There were no pets on the calendar to take care of but instead Rocky's parents invited me to join them and Rocky on a day trip to the Indiana Dunes National Park. My parents were more than happy to have time to themselves. Rocky's mom and dad explained to my parents that it was only an hour's drive away and they would have me back by dinner. Kara told me that she packed a picnic lunch and wanted me to come with to play with Rocky since her pregnancy made it difficult to run and chase dogs.

It was a beautiful day, and the Dunes were more beautiful than I ever imagined. We parked the car at the edge of a forest, and I could not see the beach or the water or the Dunes for the trees. But there was a path that meandered a short way through the forest. Rocky pulled on his leash anxious to see where the path led, and as we turned a corner, the path disappeared into an endless area of sand as far as the eye could see. Water splashed onto the nearby shore. The waves looked calm, but I could imagine that they could get bigger and more menacing without notice, and I held onto Rocky's leash a little tighter.

"What is this lake, Kara?" I asked Rocky's mother.

"That's Lake Michigan – the same lake just a mile from our building! It's huge, isn't it?" Kara said.

And I followed her gaze and saw that as large as the beach was with mounds of sand, so was the lake as it stretched out from the sandy rims of the Dunes. Rocky was not impressed. He just wanted to run. I wondered if I could keep up with him in the slippery sand. Carl, Rocky's dad, saw my distress. He turned to Kara and said, "I think we can trust Rocky to run and return to us. What do you think? Where else is he going to go?"

Kara turned to me and asked, "Do you think you can run with Rocky and guide him back to us? Maybe repeat the process a few times until he tires himself out? And then we can have lunch."

Rocky understands English. I am sure of it, because he jumped up on me handing me his leash demanding to be let go. We all laughed as he immediately took off effortlessly running down the beach and up a dune. I am glad I left on my Nikes. It was hard to keep traction in the sand. Thankfully, Rocky, who is 100 in human years, realized his age quickly and happily collapsed on the towel that Kara and Carl had unfolded on the beach. But he did not sleep. He

watched Kara's every move as she removed food from a large cooler that Carl brought from the car.

Kara made a great selection of what she called "tea" sandwiches. There was an assortment of mini-sandwiches on different kinds of breads, with different fillings like egg salad, tuna salad and chicken salad. Mind you, this meal would not be everyone's "cup of tea" but it suited me just fine. Rocky seemed content with his bone from the butcher's shop and I was content not to talk but to simply soak up the sun and pet Rocky. I realized that if my parents ever did let me have a dog, I'd want him to be exactly like Rocky. I realized in that moment how lucky I was to take care of Rocky, and it prompted me to ask Kara and Carl when they were planning their next trip. I suddenly couldn't wait to take care of Rocky again.

Kara and Carl looked at each other and didn't say anything. Oh, no. Did I say something wrong? *Something* was wrong, I could just feel it. And Rocky did too. He whined and squirmed and put his head on my lap, his drool dripping on my plate. But I didn't care. Rocky could do almost anything and not upset me.

Kara paused and then quietly said, "We need to tell you something Libby that we wish we didn't have to, but we have no choice."

Well, that wasn't much of an explanation, and it left me feeling even more uncomfortable.

Carl continued for Kara who looked like she was going to cry. "You see, Kara's pregnancy is getting to the point where she won't be able to do much that requires a lot of activity. We've been discussing moving to Seattle to be near Kara's mom and dad so that when Kara delivers, the baby will have grandparents nearby. But timing wise, we needed to move up our plans to move across the country to this month so Kara can handle packing and the trip across the country."

"You're moving?!!!" My tone made Rocky perk up his ears and bark sharply as if to say, "Don't use that tone, Libby. It's not their fault." And after giving it more than a moment of thought, I realized their moving was inevitable, but still, they were moving so quickly.

I recovered as quickly as I could and held back my tears. "I will miss you. And Rocky. I can't believe I won't take care of Rocky ever again."

"We didn't say that, Libby. How about next weekend? We aren't going anywhere but it would be so much easier to pack without Rocky underfoot. Would that work?" Carl asked.

"You bet!" Rocky was glad I had resumed a happy voice and wagged his tail, and before I could get off the blanket, he darted down the beach once again, and for the moment, as I ran after him, I was still Rocky's pet nanny.

CHAPTER 6

"Pre-School"

I had one day to myself before school started, and I expected it would fly by what with my pet sitting schedule. But it ended up there was no pet sitting schedule. My mom guessed that most people stay close to home after Labor Day and didn't need my services. I just hoped that she was right, and this wasn't the start of a slow period for The Pet Nanny, especially since Mimi had fired me and Rocky was moving.

At least Rocky was still around for now. I had such a great time with him and his pet parents at Indiana Dunes National Park. I came back on Labor Day Monday with sand EVERYWHERE. I had sand in my shoes, sand in my hair, and places I won't discuss. Kara said she had to hose Rocky down on the loading dock since he was just as sandy. Maybe my mom should have done the same with me.

My whole family was sad to hear the news that Rocky wouldn't be our house guest anymore after this coming weekend. We all agreed to make this weekend Rocky's best ever and pamper him every way we could think of. Meat bones for EVERYONE!

The Einstein/Mimi situation was not as easily handled. I hadn't run into Mimi but knew that sooner or later I should return her key. At least when I did that I could see Einstein one more time. And just as I had this thought, there was a knock at the door. I stretched on my tippy toes and peeked through the peep hole. Oh, no! It was Mimi, and since it was the middle of the morning, my parents were

working and not home. I panicked. What should I do? I really didn't want to confront Mimi without my parents there for support.

As if an answer to my prayer, I now saw George standing behind Mimi. She didn't seem to know he was there as I opened the door. I smiled (at George, not Mimi) and said, "Hey, Mimi."

Mimi was obviously confused as I continued to smile, but said quickly, "I want my key."

I ignored her request and instead said, "Oh hi, George!" Mimi quickly spun around in the direction of my gaze and lost her balance in doing so. As she tilted backwards, George steadied her by lightly gripping her shoulders.

"What are you doing George?" Mimi said accusingly.

"Well, let's see, right now I'm keeping you from falling over," George said defensively and just a little sarcastically.

"Hmmmpf. What I meant was what are you doing HERE right at this moment?" Mimi challenged George with a mean looking scowl.

"I guess I came to see Libby just like you. She needed to give you back your apartment key and I volunteered to bring it to you to avoid any awkward moments since you fired her. But I guess it's too late for that!" George said.

I used the awkward momentary silence to go fetch the key and instead of giving it directly to Mimi handed it to George who handed it to Mimi. George proclaimed, "Mission accomplished!" and turned to proceed down the hall. Mimi huffed off in the direction of her apartment and I resisted the urge to say, "Say hello to Einstein for me." Chances were I would never see Einstein again and that made me very sad.

I suddenly had an inspiration. I had most of the day ahead of me. I could go down to my "girl cave" in the basement and just hang. My refrigerator there was fully stocked with the essentials – soda and cookies – and I was pretty sure there were mini-bags of snacks on the shelves. I kept the key to my hide-a-way on a ribbon around my neck, and within moments I was uttering the secret code – Abacadabra! As I turned the key, the lights went on automatically.

"I installed an automatic motion sensor so the lights would go on the minute you opened the door and stepped in." I jumped at George's voice. I didn't realize anyone else was downstairs. But because it was George my fright was immediately replaced with a feeling of reassurance that I was safe.

"Thank you, George. That was very thoughtful. And I like the addition of the Christmas lights too!" George had strung Christmas lights along the ceiling. The different colors twinkled giving the club house a magical appearance.

George departed quickly with a "See you later, alligator!" and before I could return it with the customary "Afterwhile crocodile!", George had disappeared. I proceeded immediately to the refrigerator, grabbed a Coke and a chocolate chip cookie. Next, I looked at the books on my bookshelf (which I swore had multiplied since George first showed me the club house) and picked out an adventure book my dad had bought me at a library sale. It was a "tween" book written by one of my dad's favorite adult writers, Clive Cussler, who had decided to venture into writing children's books. The title was "Vin Fiz" and the back cover promised that it was a magical adventure taken by twelve year old twins. Just my kind of book!

I settled down for the afternoon with my snacks next to me on the table and my feet underneath me as I cuddled into the chair. The book was getting very exciting when I was startled for the second time that day by an unexpected voice. This time it was my mom reminding me it was lunch time. I reluctantly got up for a heaping helping of Tuesday's "surprise" tuna casserole. I could only hope that my mom DID surprise me with something else to eat!

CHAPTER 7

School Starts

The first day of school, no matter what grade you are in or what school you are going to, is a mixture of excitement and equal amounts of fear of the unknown. Add to it going to a brand new school in a brand new neighborhood and the experience is much more challenging.

My parents agreed that my father should drop me off and pick me up since his schedule as an insurance agent was more flexible than my mom's as a legal assistant. My mom always said the law firm owned her soul, and evidently that meant they owned her availability to be my chauffer, as well. I didn't mind that my dad would be driving me. I actually liked riding in his red convertible, especially with the top down in the warmer weather. We named my dad's car Redbird, and it lived up to its name, as my father drove fast enough to be accused of flying.

And because he drove swiftly, we arrived at school quicker than I was ready to arrive. My dad hadn't seen my school before and was impressed with its many colors. And even though the sign outside the school clearly read EDISON ELEMENTARY, my dad decided to call the school "Joseph" after Joseph and the Technicolor Dreamcoat in the Broadway play. Somehow giving the school a name helped me feel better about attending, and without looking back, I said tootles to my dad and quickly got out of the car and entered the front door of the school to be named Joseph hereafter.

I had no trouble finding my room since it was the same one my mom and I had gone to during orientation and met my teacher for the first time. I heard a lot of loud voices as I approached the room, and sure enough, as I opened the door to the room, there were many other kids my age talking in groups of two, three and one of seven! As I feared, they all seemed to know each other and I was a little intimidated as to where to go. I was contemplating turning around and going to the bathroom until the bell rang when the teacher came up and greeted me.

Just as I was returning the teacher's hello, the bell rang signaling the beginning of school. Most of the other kids just sat where they stood. I looked to the teacher for direction of where to sit and she said, "Libby, why don't you sit up here close to me at the front." And as I did the teacher rang a string of jingle bells on her desk, apparently to get everyone's attention, followed by a cowbell, and then an electronic siren. The sound of each device was louder than the last and by the time the bells stopped ringing, the room was silent. We all looked at the teacher expectantly.

"That was much more fun than screaming for you to all shut up, wasn't it?" The teacher smiled, and introduced herself. "My name is Ms. Hart, and I am very happy to be your 8th grade teacher. And without further ado, I'd like for all of us to get to know each other. Now even though many of you, strike that, most of you know each other already, it's never too late to learn more about each other. That's why I asked you to fill out the personal information sheet I gave you at Student Orientation. I trust you all came prepared?" She lifted an eyebrow and looked around the room making eye contact with each of the twenty students.

"I also want to introduce someone none of us know. She is a transfer student and new to our school. Libby, would you please bring your form to the front of the room and share your details with us?"

I blushed a bright red. I hadn't brought my form. I faced the teacher. "I didn't bring my form, but I did do the assignment. I memorized it. Is it okay if I just ad-libby it?"

I couldn't tell what the teacher was thinking, but she looked amused. I wasn't sure whether that was good or bad. She said, "Excuse me, did you say 'ad-libby'?"

I couldn't believe she didn't know the meaning of the word.

"Libby, I think you mean 'adlib' which means a speech made without preparation," Ms. Hart said with a slight smile.

"Oh, I see your confusion," I said confidently. "If just anyone speaks off the cuff, then they adlib. But when I do it, it's "Ad-libbying".

Ms. Hart laughed and said, "Then by all means, 'ad-libby' away!"

I stood at the front of the room and introduced myself. "Hello fellow classmates. My name is Libby Lancaster. My parents and I moved at the start of the summer to downtown Chicago from Palos Heights in the southwest suburbs. I thought very hard about what three words I would use to describe myself, and I finally came up with likable (and I hope you all agree after you get to know me), lucky (because I am lucky to be here), and lazy (because my mother is always complaining that I forget to do my chores). I just turned thirteen on August 30th and my parents gave me a surprise birthday party and invited thirteen guests – including a dog! Speaking of dogs, playing with cats and dogs is my FAVORITE thing to do. I also like to read and hang out in my personal clubhouse in the basement of our apartment building. My favorite wild animal is a giraffe. I think they are beautiful and graceful. Here's three facts everyone should know about giraffes: they are vegetarians; they travel in packs called 'towers'; and they can run 35 miles per hour. For now, my favorite song is Flashing Lights by Kanye West but that could change as quick as a giraffe can run because I love all kinds of music."

I went to sit down, but the teacher said, "One more thing, Libby. Since you proved yourself good at ad-libbying I'd like you to also share what you did over the summer. Just a heads-up to the rest of you, I am going to ask you each to do the same thing when it is your turn."

I was taken aback for a minute. I had no problem sharing to a point, but at school orientation my mom said not to mention my pet sitting business. But since that was how I spent my summer

vacation, didn't I have to share now? Besides, she didn't say anything this morning about not sharing NOW. Decision made! I was happy to share that I was the Pet Nanny!

I resumed my position at the front of the class. I started with the title of my presentation. "How I spent my summer vacation: My father and I went to Wisconsin Dells, Wisconsin and did all the usual things you do there like ride the Ducks, went to the water parks, and played miniature golf. Then just a few days ago I went with my friends and their dog Rocky to Indiana Dunes National Park for the day at the beach. But I spent the entire summer running my own pet business. I watch five dogs and three cats in the apartment building where I live. And did I mention, I do it for money? That's it. That's how I spent my summer vacation."

Whew. I was glad I could remember all that after I bragged about ad-libbying, but it seemed the rest of the class enjoyed it because they all clapped at the end, and didn't clap again until the fourth or fifth girl stood up and handed out candy to everyone when she announced one of her favorite things was to eat Smarty Candies. And to drive home the point one of her words that described her was "smart". Since her name was Suzy she had to come up with three things that started with an 'S'. I think it was more likely 'Smarty Pants'. I hate to say this, but I took an instant dislike to Suzy Smarty Pants, probably because I think she got more applause than I did.

I finally took out my notebook and took notes on each of my classmates and wrote a short description of each so I could remember them better. After a while, they all looked alike, especially since we all wore the same uniform. We were only through half the class when the teacher rang the cowbell, signalling a short "recess". It was already 9:30 a.m. Since we were on split shifts with the morning shift ending at noon, we didn't get an outdoor recess or a lunch, but the teacher said we could use this time to eat a piece of fruit she provided at the back of the room, and a bottle of iced water.

All that adlibbying made me hungry but when I got to the back of the room, I was surrounded by a group of my classmates. I thought they wanted to hear about my pet sitting business. But no. They wanted to know how it was to ride a duck, and how did I make sure they didn't fly away, and how big were these ducks anyway? I explained that the Ducks weren't real ducks, they were boats named The Ducks, and Suzy Smarty Pants hmpffed and said, "Well why didn't you just say so?"

Yep. It's official. I don't like Suzy Smarty Pants.

CHAPTER 8

First Day Down

The rest of the day passed without incident. Most of the other kids' questionnaire answers and summer vacation reports were kind of boring and repeated the same travel destination. Just how many people take cruises and trips to Greece? And, here's my question, WHY? They don't even have Ducks!

My dad picked me up promptly at noon in Redbird, and asked me the inevitable question: "So how was school today?"

"I don't know dad. How was work?" I know I was being sarcastic, but honestly, why does every parent think this is a mandatory after-school question opener for every student across the world?

He let it pass. Dad is good that way. Not so much Mom. She was waiting at home with a special "first day of school" lunch. It was one of my favorites – a chicken gyros sandwich with extra tzatziki sauce and fries from Mr. Gyros. But when she asked the question "So how was school today?", she earned the one word answer, "Fine." Come on, she earned it. No one makes gyros like Mr. Gyros.

My mother looked across the table at my father, rolled her eyes, and sighed. My father shrugged. Whatever.

After both my parents went back to work, I labored like Cinderella cleaning the kitchen. (Meaning I threw out the wrappers in the bag the food was delivered in) and decided to throw the bag out at the garbage bins on the loading dock since gyros remnants can be kind of stinky. On the way, I ran into George, who asked, YOU GUESSED IT!, "So how was school today?" But somehow when

George asked the question, it sounded more like, "Welcome home, Libby. I missed you today and I'm extremely interested in hearing how your first day at your new school went."

And so George got three words, "It was ok." With a smile. I would have said more, but we were interrupted by the beeper on his phone alerting him to a tenant emergency.

I decided to go down to my clubhouse after throwing out the garbage. I went down the stairs, input the secret 1234 code on the outer door, and retrieved my key from inside my blouse while uttering Abacadabra as I opened the door. Maybe I should have changed from my uniform. I pledged to try to remember that in the future.

I promptly fetched a soda from the refrigerator and sank into my comfy chair. The book I was reading was already in place on the table next to my chair. I cracked open the Coke, opened the book to a new chapter, and promptly fell asleep. Evidently listening to all those other kids prattle on was more exhausting than I thought. When I heard my mom's voice calling me to dinner three hours had gone by. This school thing took more energy than I remember, and now I had pets to watch too. Time to summon my inner Super Thirteen-Year-Old!

And none too soon as my mom consulted her email. She had received several messages from pet parents scheduling The Pet Nanny for the coming week, including Rocky this weekend. My mom frowned as she read the messages aloud, as Anita, mother of three dogs, Buddy, Brownie and Blaze, and my very first Pet Nanny customer, wanted me to walk her dogs at 8 a.m. each day the following week. Of course, my school schedule prevented that from happening as I started school at 7 a.m. and had to leave no later than 6:45 a.m. to arrive on time. The other requests were from cat owners who were much more flexible. Notably missing was a message from Mimi, Einstein's mother, who fired me earlier in the week. I had hoped she would change her mind, but it appeared she did not.

My mom and dad looked at each other. My dad cleared his throat and said, "Libby, I think we have to talk about the practicality of your keeping up the Pet Nanny business. It was one thing this summer when you were on summer vacation, but now your number one priority has to be school. You do understand that, right?"

I couldn't believe my parents didn't even try to see that this situation could be worked out and immediately jumped to the conclusion that I couldn't watch the pets I had grown to love, let alone the money I earned from watching them.

"I think we have options here," I said with hope in my voice. "What if I ask Anita if I could take the dogs out at 6 a.m.? I could get ready for school before I take them, and even if they took a longer walk than usual, I'd be back way before it was time to leave?"

"And when will you take care of the cats?" my mom asked.

"If it is only one or two, I can do that before I leave as well, and then again before dinner. Please let me try," I begged.

"And Rocky? What about him?" my dad added, trying to rock the boat.

"He's not until the weekend, and I am pretty sure we won't be watching him again before they move." I countered.

My parents hesitated but before giving in, insisted that I leave a note for each of my customers telling them that I had started school, and now had to conform to a new schedule. I agreed, but knew I had to talk to Anita immediately to get her permission to take out her three dogs at 6 a.m. I couldn't see why that would be a problem.

But it was. Anita answered at the first knock and was happy to see me. She was just contemplating taking the dogs out but was tired and really didn't look forward to it. I volunteered to do it for free, mainly just to postpone my talk with her. I saddled up the puppies with their harnesses and leashes and took my time walking them around the block. For once, none of them pooped. I would have even welcomed picking up their poop just to buy a few extra minutes.

Finally, I asked Anita if she had a minute to talk with me after I unleashed the hounds. She motioned to a seat on the couch and the dogs jumped up on either side of me, jockeying for positions to be petted. I knew I had to come out with it, so I came right to the point. "I don't know if you know this, Anita, but I started back to school this week. I have the early shift which means I will be going to school from 7 a.m. to noon. I know you wanted me to take out the

pups at 8 a.m. but I obviously can't. Would it be okay with you if I took them out at 6 a.m.?"

Anita looked at me as if I had asked for the moon. She hesitated and then said, "I'm sure the dogs wouldn't mind but I get my best sleep those last two hours before 6 a.m. and 8 a.m. I can't imagine having to wake up to greet you any earlier than 8 a.m."

"What if you didn't get up at all? Your dogs are not really barkers. I could just let myself in and take them out real quiet like." I hated that I sounded so needy but after Mimi fired me, I felt like I couldn't bear it if I lost another customer. The puppies must have felt my fear because they looked at Anita with the same expressions they used when begging for treats.

"Well, I can't say no to all four of you, so okay, for now. We'll see how it goes." Anita looked less than convinced but I assured her I wouldn't let her down.

The subject didn't come up again that night when I returned home and that night when I went to bed I wondered if every school day was going to be this long and tiring.

CHAPTER 9

A New Friend

Dad roared up to the entrance of the school the next day and I had to wonder, not for the first time, why some people thought it was necessary to announce their entrance with loud motor sounds. And just as I had this thought, a nearby group of boys gazed over to see what car made such a big noise. Oh, no! I recognized these boys. They were in my class. I quickly got out of the car and walked in a big circle around where the boys stood. Oh no! One of the boys was walking toward me.

"Hey, Libby," the boy said. Was he talking to me? How did he know my name? What were the chances that there was another Libby around?

For the first time I looked at who it was. I remembered this boy. When he read his information sheet yesterday, I remember he said some personal details that I thought were actually interesting and I remember specifically he was the only boy that didn't include sports in his profile of what he liked to do.

Just in time I remembered his first name: Steve. "Oh, hi Steve." That's me. The conversationalist!

"Hey, is that your car?" he said pointing in the direction of my dad and Redbird.

Oh, he sounded like he liked the car. "Well, it's my dad's." I looked at my dad frantically waving goodbye, waiting for me to acknowledge him so that he could drive off to work.

I gave a short wave and to my horror my dad blew me a kiss. Maybe Steve didn't notice. If he did, he didn't mention it. "I like convertibles. I especially like the Mustang GT convertible. Bet you can't wait to drive it in a few years, right?"

"Yah, right. Well, off to class. I don't want to be late," I said as I made my great escape. I practically ran inside, and once I was outside the classroom I wondered why I rushed. I actually enjoyed talking to Steve.

I got another chance almost immediately. When the classroom started filling up Steve took the empty seat next to mine.

"Did you have as hard a time as I did completing that personal information questionnaire? After I heard your answers, I thought, 'hey! I like to read and play with dogs and cats too. I found it really hard to limit my favorite things to do list to three things." He looked at me expectantly.

"I remember you like cars, and now I know you especially like Mustang convertibles. But what were your other favorite things?" I asked.

"I listed Bird Watching and Photography," Steve replied. "Do you like either of those?"

"Well actually, my dad is a big bird watcher. When we lived in Palos Heights he used to go every Sunday morning with a bird watcher group. But now that he moved downtown, he hasn't gone. I know he misses it."

Steve took out a piece of paper and was writing on it. When he was done, he handed me the slip of paper. "This is the name of a bird watching group in the downtown Chicago area. I am its youngest member. We meet every Saturday morning at 8 a.m. at Jackson Park. It's right by the Museum of Science and Industry. Any chance you and your dad could join us tomorrow? It would be great to have someone my age in the group. Most of the people are really old like our parent's age."

"Thanks for the info. I know my dad will be really excited to resume his weekend bird watching. But unfortunately, I am watching a dog named Rocky this weekend. Hey, any chance we could bring Rocky along?" I asked.

"Sorry, no puppies allowed. They scare off the birds. But maybe another weekend when you don't have Rocky to watch you can watch birds with your dad and me." Steve said encouragingly. I liked that he left the opportunity open and wondered if I would like watching birds. Frankly, it always seemed like it would be a boring thing to do. But maybe not if Steve would be there.

My pondering over the possibilities ended when the bell rang, and only then did I notice all the helium balloons at the front of the classroom.

"Hey," I whispered to Steve. "What's up with the balloons?"

"Beats me," Steve shrugged his shoulders. "Maybe we are celebrating someone's birthday?"

Before we could speculate more, Ms. Hart rang the three bells in sequence as she did the day before. And just like the previous day, everyone quieted down immediately.

"Welcome, class and happy Friday! You are probably all wondering what is going on with the balloons, and no, it's not my birthday! At orientation, I told each of you and your parents that on Fridays we would reverse roles, and you would be the teachers of a specific topic for the day. These helium balloons contain slips of paper with different assignments within a single topic. The pink balloons include assignments for the "Famous Hero" topic. The white balloons include assignments for the "Inventor" topic. I will call each of you up here to pop either a white balloon or a pink balloon. If you don't like the assignment you "popped", then you may pop one other balloon of a different color. You will then put your rejected assignment on my desk, keeping the white and pink balloon assignments separate. After the first person has rejected an assignment, if the next person also wants an opportunity to pick another assignment, they can either pop a balloon or pick one of the rejected slips on the desk.

On the next two Fridays, each of you will make a presentation on your assignment selection. Next Friday will be Famous Heroes day and the following Friday will be Inventors. You will limit your presentation to ten minutes, so that at the end of the day we will hear from each of you on the given topic. And even though technically you are the teacher for the day, you will still be graded.

I know this sounds confusing but trust me it's simple and I'm here to help you through it. And if you keep an open mind, this can

be fun – more like a game than a boring school assignment. I will call you up alphabetically by first name, so keep an ear open for me to call your name. In the meantime, I have a surprise for each of you. The Literacy Foundation donated a copy of a book for each of you that I think you'll enjoy. It's The Swiss Family Robinson. I'm going to pass the books around, and I encourage you to start reading the book while your classmates are getting their assignments."

Ms. Hart proceeded to give each of us the book The Swiss Family Robinson, which I had heard about but never read. When she came to my desk, I asked, "Is this ours for keeps?" She nodded yes and continued with her task. I immediately started reading, and even the sound of the popping balloons did not disrupt my attention to the book. What did startle me was the booming voice of George's brother Jerry, the vice principal, who opened the classroom door loudly questioning "What is the loud sounds I can hear all the way down the hall to my office?"

Ms. Hart laughed. I loved her laugh. "Now, Mr. Vice Principal, don't tell me you can't recognize the sound of a popping balloon?"

"And exactly why are you popping balloons instead of studying quietly?" the vice principal demanded.

"Because one is fun, and the other isn't?" Ms. Hart said it so sweetly the vice principal had no alternative but to accept her answer and go back to his office. But before he did, he came over to my desk and crouched down.

He whispered softly, "Libby, after you pop your balloon, will you please come down to my office?" I was equally mortified as to the reason the vice principal wanted to see me and curious as to why I would be singled out.

And I also wondered not for the first time and not for the last time how George and Vice Principal Jerry could be related. Maybe Jerry was adopted.

Before I could return to reading the antics of the Robinson family, Ms. Hart called me up to pop my balloon. I noticed there were quite a few rejected slips of paper for both topics, but first I needed to see if I liked my balloon option. And I did! The slip in my pink balloon read: FAMOUS HERO: JOAN OF ARC. I was ecstatic. Getting to research this saint would be a pleasure, but I wondered how I could limit my comments to ten minutes. I couldn't wait to get started.

Before Ms. Hart could call up the next student, I told her that the vice principal wanted to see me. She immediately inquired whether everything was okay, but she did it with a slight smile. My Spidey senses were already tingling, but Ms. Hart made them explode. I answered honestly, "I hope so. But I better go and find out, right?"

Ms. Hart nodded, and I was off dragging my feet the few feet down the hall to Vice Principal Jerry's office, fearful as to why he wanted to see me.

I knocked on his door and I heard two sounds answer simultaneously – the Vice Principal's and a cat's meow. I opened the door cautiously and saw Jerry sitting behind his desk holding and petting the cat I rescued at Orientation.

Jerry motioned that I should close the door behind me and sit down across the desk from him and the kitty. I couldn't take my eyes off the beautiful green-eyed kitty and couldn't resist asking, "Can I pet him? Or is it a her?"

Jerry looked at me as if he never bothered to find out whether it was a boy or a girl kitty and held the cat up for me to see its underside. "Oh," I sighed. For some reason, I pictured it a lady cat, but it was a boy. Oh well, it was still irresistible, and without further ado, Jerry handed over the boy cat to be petted.

"What's his name?" was my next question.

"How should I know?" Jerry replied in the grumpy tone I remembered all too well from Orientation.

"Well, what do you call it?" I asked to which Jerry shrugged.

I sat the cat up so that Jerry could study him. "What do you think he looks like?"

Jerry took a quick glance and said, "I'm no good at naming. You name it. It's partly why I asked you in here anyway."

I smiled at my good fortune. I love naming things. I name everything – cars, pets, even furniture! It came to me in a millisecond. "Henry!" I exclaimed without further explanation.

And just as quickly Henry's owner nodded and said, "Agreed!" Little did I know that morning when I woke up I was going to name a cat. "You said there was another reason you asked me to come to your office?"

I held my breath expecting there could still be some horrible thing he wanted to share. I was pleasantly surprised. "Libby, I'm new to this pet thing and George says you are an expert. It's obvious Henry likes you." On cue Henry purred and snuggled in my arms. "I'd like your help in taking care of Henry during the school week. What do you think?"

What do I think? I think YES!!! But wait…. not so fast. How was that going to work? I asked the obvious question. "So how do you envision me going to school AND taking care of Henry?"

"I already talked with Ms. Hart. She said she will discretely excuse you from class on the ruse of using the bathroom. Then instead of going to the bathroom, you can come to my office, feed the cat, give It a few cuddles and go back to class. Easy-peasy!" Jerry actually looked proud of himself.

I hesitated. This certainly wasn't normal school protocol. "I will have to ask my parent's permission," I said half-heartedly. *Did I?, I wondered.*

"Already done! George asked them for me and they agreed but they wanted to leave the final decision up to you." Again, Jerry sat back with a look of pride.

"Well, then, you have a deal," and I gave Henry a smooch to seal the deal. And just like that The Pet Nanny expanded services to a second location.

I reluctantly handed Henry back to Jerry and turned to leave the office. "One more thing before you go." My heart dropped. Oh, no. Here it comes. I knew this couldn't be that easy. "Even though Ms. Hart knows our arrangement, I would like to keep this under wraps from everyone else in the school. Some may not view it kosher, if you know what I mean."

Actually, I had no idea what "kosher" was – except for a word I heard at Manny's, my favorite Jewish deli in downtown Chicago. But I think I got the gist of what he was saying. I was to keep taking care of Henry our secret. I put my fingers to my lips and made the universal locking gesture that his secret was safe with me. And quickly before he could change his mind, I fled his office. I felt like I was away from my classroom for hours, but it was actually only a few minutes. I felt guilty for some reason, a natural feeling for most people with a mandatory visit to the vice principal's office. But I also felt a surge of pleasure at my secret mission – Code Word HENRY.

The remaining children were still selecting their assignments and before I knew it, the last balloon was popped. Not everyone looked as happy with their choice as I was, but maybe they would change their minds after reading up on their heroes and inventors.

Ms. Hart rang the cow bell to get our attention. "I apologize that we didn't get a break today." I looked up at the clock and was amazed to see the time. It was five minutes to twelve! Ms. Hart continued, "Please grab a banana on your way out and enjoy your weekend. If you can, get started on your assignments. On Monday, the whole school will start the day with an assembly in our gymnasium. Our vice principal has lots of announcements to make and you won't want to miss a minute! Normal classes will start immediately afterwards. Also, please bring your notebook and pen, as well as your laptop. Make sure it's charged! We will start with your regular lessons on Monday. I can't wait!" Ms. Hart sounded genuinely enthusiastic. I hoped some of her attitude would rub off on me when it came to Math.

Steve and I left the classroom at the same time and grabbed bananas on our way out. "Wait a minute, there's writing on mine. Is there on yours?" Steve asked and as I glanced down at the banana, I laughed.

"Yes, it says, 'You are appealing'. Get it, a-peel-ing – like a banana peel? It's like Ms. Hart prepared fruit fortune cookies for us! She's the best, don't you think?" I asked.

"If you say so. I don't like what I picked. Who did you get?" Steve frowned.

"I got Joan of Arc for a hero. I guess I should say heroine. I'm excited! Who did you get?" I couldn't imagine why Steve wouldn't be happy.

"I picked a white balloon because I like inventors, but I picked Thomas Alva Edison – the guy our school is named after. I like Edison but it's a lot of pressure having only ten minutes to talk about

him. Before we could discuss this dilemma further, I heard my dad honking the horn, trying to hurry me along, no doubt.

"See you, Steve."

"See you, Libby. Have a good weekend."

"You too," I turned to smile at Steve but stopped short when I saw Smarty Pants Suzy siddling up to Steve.

One more loud honk from my dad stopped me from staring further, but it ended my school day on a sour note. I couldn't say why, but I didn't like her talking to Steve. At all.

CHAPTER 10

A Rocky Weekend

As soon as I got home, my parents and I had lunch from McDonalds. I am always happy with McDonalds, even though I outgrew Happy Meals a long time ago. I let out a yelp when I opened my bag. "A McRib! Mom, how did you get a McRib? I thought they only made it once in a great while."

"Well, this must be time for a great while because they offered it, and I grabbed it knowing you like the sandwich so well. Your Dad got his boring Friday favorite, a fish sandwich." My Mom grimaced when she handed my dad his sandwich. She did not like fish. At all. And that made my mind drift to Suzy Smarty Pants who I did not like. At all. And involuntarily I made the same face as my mom.

"What, you don't like fish either? Since when?" My dad and mom were looking at me critically.

"No, I like fish fine, but I don't like this girl in my class that reminds me of a fish." That wasn't exactly right, but close enough to the truth and about all I wanted to say on the subject. But, oops! I opened the door to the classic question about what was going on at school.

Without skipping a beat, my mom started in. "It's only the second day of school and already you don't like someone? That's not like you, Libby. Did this girl say or do something to upset you?"

"Not exactly, she just has an attitude that I don't like." I had to divert this conversation quickly. And then the perfect topic came to me.

"Dad, there is a boy in my class who listed bird watching as one of his favorite activities and he asked if I liked birds, and of course, I

told him no, but that my dad did and he wrote you this note about a bird watching group he is a member of and they meet on Saturdays at 8 a.m. in Jackson Park and I kinda said you might be there tomorrow because I know you miss going bird watching." My lungs ran out of air. Whew! I took in a deep breath and handed my dad Steve's note. "What do you think?"

"Never mind for a minute what your dad thinks. I want to know more about this *boy* in your class," my mother said with a smirk. Argh. I hated that smirk.

One look at my dad and I knew he understood or at least sympathized. "You know Libby, I think it's a great idea. I'd love to go tomorrow morning. What did you say this boy's name was?"

"Yes, what did you say *his* name was?" my mother smirked AGAIN.

"Steve. His name is Steve." Quick Libby – time for another conversation changer. And then it came to me.

"Guess what!" I said with as much enthusiasm as I could muster. "We picked our topics we need to present over the next two Fridays and I got Joan of Arc as my heroine."

"But Libby, we aren't even Catholic. Whyever did you choose Joan of Arc? My mom looked at me with disappointment. "But your father might as well be the way he insists eating fish on Fridays." And with that the conversation turned to a disagreement between my parents regarding his eating habits, and I was off the hook, at least for the moment.

A familiar knock at the door and bark outside was another welcome diversion. I knew it must be Rocky. "Hi, George. Hi, Rocky!" I exclaimed as I gave Rocky a big hug.

"Are you ready for your weekend with Rocky?" George asked as he passed me the tote bag that served as Rocky's suitcase.

"I sure am, George, but I thought I was supposed to pick up Rocky later this afternoon?" I wondered if I missed an email, or simply forgot the plan. Either way, I was disappointed in myself and my mother, the official scheduler.

"You are correct, but then Kara called me and asked if I could bring Rocky and his packed bag over earlier so she and Carl could spend the afternoon finishing some errands. You know how unhappy Rocky gets if left alone too long," George explained. And, oh boy, did I know. Rocky could howl with the best of wolves.

"Well, thank you for fetching him," I said as I unhooked Rocky's leash. Rocky made a run for the bathroom to shred up toilet paper and empty the wastepaper basket. I quickly ran after him, and when I got back a moment later George had done his famous disappearing act.

My mom and dad were looking at me strangely. They didn't look happy. My mom spoke first. "Just how long is Rocky here for?" Nope, she definitely wasn't happy.

"The weekend. Remember Kara and Carl needed the weekend to pack and get ready to move and they wanted Rocky out of the way. This is probably our last chance to take care of Rocky before they move." How could they forget such a momentous occasion?

Only they hadn't forgotten. I had forgotten to tell them. Oops. This managing school and the pet nanny business was a little challenging, and it had only been a few days since I had to do both. I needed to step up my game, especially when starting Monday I had several dogs and cats to take care of. Did I forget to tell my parents about that as well?

CHAPTER 11

There's No Business Like Pet Business

"So, Libby, your dad and I wanted to talk to you about this upcoming week," my mom hesitated as she looked over to my dad for support. This didn't look good.

It was Sunday night and Rocky just left with his pet parents, Kara and Carl. It had been an exhausting weekend since I had to do most of the work with Rocky. Which is only fair since I am the Pet Nanny, but would it have killed my dad not to start his bird watching in Jackson Park THIS Saturday? He was gone most of the day and all he had to report was the sighting of pink flamingoes which blew in on stormy winds from Florida. Oh, and also the "sighting" of Steve, my classmate who is also an avid bird watcher. That was slightly more interesting, even though my father didn't share much information.

And would it have killed my mother to skip an all-day trek to Costco for her monthly shopping spree, followed by having her nails done?

Thank goodness for George who at least provided some human companionship in the hallway when I took Rocky in and out for his walks and bathroom trips. But even George wasn't available much as his duties at the loading dock were required. The building had two move-ins this weekend. I wanted to find out more information about who was moving in. Specifically, I wanted to know if they had pets that needed a sitter, but I was shooshed by George to get out of the way. I would have been insulted by anyone else but not by George.

Oops. My mom had been talking and I was daydreaming again. I tried to focus on what my mother was saying, prompted by her insistent, "Libby, Libby, earth to Libby." I had to watch my attention span. She had to use that phrase way too often.

'Your dad and I were talking about what will be required of you, and possibly us, in the upcoming weeks, and frankly, we do not think it is going to work." Mom paused and looked at me closely. *What, did I have a zit? Why is she looking at me like that... and what was that she was saying? Something about something not working?*

"What's not working? Can't George fix it?" I asked, knowing that whatever wasn't working, George could fix it.

My mom looked at my dad, evidently for help since I obviously wasn't paying close enough attention to know what my mom was talking about.

"Libby, what your mom is trying to say is that The Pet Nanny is on probation. We are going to closely monitor you, your schoolwork, and the pet nanny business for the next two weeks, and if we see your schoolwork failing, AT ALL, you will have to tell the pet owners you can no longer care for their pets." My dad reached out to grab my hand in reassurance, but I ran down the hallway instead and slammed my door. I fell on top of my Hello Kitty coverlet and covered my head with the matching Hello Kitty pillow and cried myself to sleep.

I awoke when my mom announced from the bedroom door that Sunday night pizza was ready. I LOVED Sunday night pizza, but not tonight. I told my mom "No, thank you," and closed my eyes for a fitful night of sleep.

CHAPTER 12

A Bad Beginning

After tossing and turning all night, sunlight finally streamed through the window. Without opening my eyes, I tried to determine what day of the week it was and what I should be doing. It came to me slowly by recounting what my latest memories were. Let's see, the last thing I remembered was the weekend with Rocky, and how sad I felt when Rocky left knowing it was the last time I would take care of him before he moved.

No, that wasn't quite right. I remembered something else... I remembered smelling delicious pizza, but I didn't remember eating it. That's strange, I thought. And then it came to me. I didn't eat the pizza because I was pouting in bed. And then I remembered my parents' heart-to-heart talk about being on Pet Nanny probation. With a start I sat up straight in bed. It was Monday morning. I had school today but first I had to check on Charley and Felix, the cats, and walk Buddy, Brownie and Blaze at 6 a.m.

My heart raced as I grabbed the Hello Kitty alarm clock next to my bed. It blinked over and over 4:00 a.m. 4:00 a.m. 4:00 a.m. But the sunlight indicated it was much later. What happened? And just as I was struggling to understand what was going on my bedroom door slammed open.

"Libby, get up! Get up! We had a storm last night and we lost electricity." My mom consulted her watch and said, "It's 6:25. If you get up right away and wash your face, brush your teeth and put on your uniform, your dad can get you to school on time!"

"But mom, I promised Anita I would walk the dogs, and I have to feed Charley and Felix and change their litter box. I'll just have to be late for school." I silently begged her to understand, but knew this was exactly what my parents were saying last night, and I unwittingly violated my own Pet Nanny probation.

"I'm afraid not. School is your priority. Your dad or I will take care of the pets. Move it! Now!" I knew my mother's different voice tones. This was the one that meant there was no debate. Twenty minutes later my dad and I were leaving the apartment when I heard multiple barks around the corner. As we headed to the garage, there was George in the hallway with Buddy, Brownie and Blaze.

"I thought you might have overslept because of the storm last night and the electricity going out. I grabbed the three amigos here and took them on a long walk. And when I return them to Anita, I'll take care of Felix and Charley. Any other cats or dogs needing attention this morning, Libby?" George looked at me as if he knew the answer. I was so grateful to him, I just shook my head, no.

"Thanks George. You're a lifesaver!" My dad said to George and gave me a gentle push in the direction of the garage, and we stepped up our pace. I didn't want to be late for school and add that to my offenses.

CHAPTER 13

Monday, Monday

As we drove up to the school there was a long line of cars letting kids off at the curb. We found out later that much of the surrounding neighborhood, including ours, had an electric outage overnight. In fact, it was one of the biggest outages in recent years due to a generator station being hit by lightning. I barely let my dad stop before opening the door and scooting in the front door of the school, remembering at the last minute that we were having an assembly today and all grades were meeting in the auditorium. I headed in that direction trying to spot Steve so we could sit together. Instead, I ran into Jerry, the vice principal, who stepped in front of me so swiftly that I almost ran into him.

"Good morning," I said pleasantly trying to slide between Jerry and the wall.

"Thank God you're on time," Jerry said. I thought to myself *what does that mean?*

"George says you are a talented pianist," Jerry said in a tone partially statement, partially question.

"I know how to play, if that's what you mean," I said cautiously. I wondered where we were going with this line of questioning.

"Great. Follow me," Jerry instructed as he led me into the auditorium and toward the front of the stage. Crowds of students parted ways so that we could walk through them easily. I felt like Moses and the Red Sea.

"Here's the deal," explained Jerry.

"Mrs. Lucifer. Yes, that's her actual name. Very unfortunate, I know. Anyway, Mrs. Lucifer is suffering from hot flashes and couldn't be here today. She always provides whatever piano accompaniment we might need here at the school. So today we need you to step up, literally onto the stage, and play the Star-Spangled Banner at the start of the assembly, after we recite The Pledge of Allegiance."

I was looking at the ancient piano and wondered how long it was here. Probably at least as long as Jerry. I lifted the lid of the piano bench looking for music, and there was none. "Eh, Jerry, there's no sheet music in here," I said, afraid of his answer.

It was as I feared. "Of course not. Every pianist worth their salt knows The Star-Spangled Banner. Don't *you*?" Well, I did but if I had known ahead of time, I would have at least practiced to make sure I remembered it.

Jerry didn't wait for my answer. Instead, he made a bad situation even worse. "Oh, and here's a microphone. Let me adjust it to your height." Jerry adjusted a microphone to tilt lower than it had been, and motioned for me to sit down at the piano. "We'll need you to lead the song as well. I trust this isn't a problem. Just use the sweet voice you use with Henry the cat, not the one you use with adults." And with that Jerry disappeared just like his brother George often does.

I stared out at the auditorium. It was almost filled with students, and I felt like each one was leering at me. I heard Jerry's voice welcoming the students to Second Monday of the Month Assembly and directing them to stand and say The Pledge of Allegiance. And then the moment I dreaded. Jerry was now telling them to continue standing while Edison Elementary's newest student, Libby Lancaster, would play AND sing the Star-Spangled Banner.

My inner pianist kicked into automatic mode, even though I hadn't played a piano since I moved from Palos Heights three months ago and left behind my baby grand. My inner singer was a bit more shy and took a few seconds to get up to the correct volume, but after a few words everyone joined in and my voice was drowned out by the others. And before you could say:

> Say, can you see
> By the dawn's early light
> What so proudly we hailed
> At the twilight's last gleaming?
> Whose broad stripes and bright stars
> Through the perilous fight
> O'er the ramparts we watched
> Were so gallantly, yeah, streaming?
> And the rockets' red glare
> The bombs bursting in air
> Gave proof through the night
> That our flag was still there
> O say, does that star-spangled banner yet wave
> O'er the land of the free and the home of the brave.

…the song was over! I considered getting off the stage for the remainder of the assembly but didn't trust my wobbly legs, so I stayed put and listened to Jerry drone on about Edison Elementary and how it was a school devoted to creativity. Blah blah blah.

But then he said something that perked my interest. He was announcing that for 7th and 8th graders only there were extracurricular activities available after school. One of the activities was Debate Club. I loved being in Debate Club last year at my old school. I was definitely going to join Debate Club. I couldn't wait to sign up. I never once thought I needed to check with my folks, or the cats and dogs that depended on me getting right home from school. I was about to commit another strike on my Pet Nanny probation.

A few more announcements and assembly was dismissed. I was pleasantly surprised to find Steve waiting for me to walk back to class. "Wow! You play great and you sing good too," Steve said, causing me to blush a bright burning red. *Oh no, I thought. I think I caught Mrs. Lucifer's hot flashes!*

CHAPTER 14

Class Begins

The trio of Ms. Hart's bells were ringing when we entered the classroom. Steve and I took our seats next to each other and Ms. Hart welcomed us back to our second week of school. Ms. Hart remarked that before announcing our subjects today she first wanted to ask the new school pianist to stand up and for the rest of the class to clap.

Wow! I thought. I only played for the first time this morning and already I was replaced? A moment later Steve poked me gently and whispered, "Libby, stand up! The class is clapping for you!"

Oh, that was embarrassing, I thought. But nobody seemed to notice and I gave a little curtsy. I didn't know what else to do in this circumstance but somehow above the noise of the others clapping I distinctly heard Suzy Smarty Pants snickering. Nope, I don't like her. At all.

The moment of fame was brief. Now Ms. Hart was talking about Math and English and Science and other stuff I really didn't have much interest in. I'd quickly learn that this litany of subjects would be repeated every day, Monday through Thursday, for the rest of the semester and I predicted that I wouldn't like them much more at the end of the semester than I did now at the beginning. Hopefully learning would come as naturally to me at Edison Elementary as it did at my old school.

I looked at the clock and was amazed to see two hours had gone by. I didn't have to fake the need to go to the bathroom in order to go

see Henry the cat. I raised my hand and Ms. Hart simply nodded. I made a quick pit stop at the bathroom and then a few doors down to Jerry's office. I knocked on the door but no one answered so I gently opened the door and immediately spied Henry sprawled on top of Jerry's desk on a stack of files. He picked up a paw as if to wave hello when I came in, as I gently closed the door behind me.

"Good morning, Henry. How are you? How was your weekend? I missed you." Henry purred in response to both my words and to my stroking his fur. He especially liked when I pet him on his forehead and between his eyes. After a few minutes I located Henry's bowl and poured some food in it. He quickly jumped off the desk and rubbed my legs until the coast was clear to his dish. Then it was all about the food. Henry didn't even glance my way as I left the office and returned to the classroom.

I didn't miss much. I quickly caught up with some math aptitude problems Ms. Hart gave each of us to determine where we were on the math learning curve. After everyone was done we were able to self-score as Ms. Hart called out the answers. Both Steve and I had the same results! I don't know why but that made me feel good. The blush returned. Maybe it was just hot in the classroom.

Class was over before I could look at the clock again. Steve walked me to the curb where my Dad was waiting. "Hi, Mr. Lancaster. How you doin'?" Steve asked my dad.

"Great, Steve. Hey, thanks again for letting me know about the bird watching group. I really enjoyed myself on Saturday. And how about those flamingos, huh?" My dad actually talked to Steve like a regular person, not a 13-year-old. I felt left out when I realized they both forgot I was even standing there.

Another car honked behind my dad and I and Steve quickly said their goodbyes. "Tootles, Steve," I said regretfully. I wish we had more time to talk but another honk and my dad motioned that I should get in the car. I barely had my seatbelt on when my dad sped away but not before I saw Steve in the rearview mirror with his hand raised to say goodbye and the same look of regret I had on my face. And somehow that made me feel better, as I blushed again, Alright, this blushing thing was getting old.

My dad and I had didn't talk much on the way home. I wondered if I was in trouble and then I remembered how the day started out. It seemed so long ago but memories of this morning came back in a rush. Memories of how I failed to walk Blaze and his brothers, and how I didn't have time to look in on Felix and Charley. Ruh roh! As Scooby Doo would say every time he encountered a problem. This morning's events certainly qualified as a major Ruh roh!

My mom was waiting for my dad and me. She had already put lunch on the table. It was peanut butter and jelly sandwiches, which she only made when she was not happy with me. At least she was courteous enough not to say anything until we had all finished our sandwiches, but somehow even a glass of milk didn't seem to accomplish my swallowing the sticky peanut butter. Fear and peanut butter stuck in my throat.

My mom cleared her throat. Evidently, she did not have the same problem with peanut butter. "Well, Libby, I was glad to hear from George who heard from Jerry that not only did you make it to school on time, but you also were the star of the day playing the piano. I hope you enjoyed it because your fame is not shared here at home."

Okay, mom, just come out with it. You're mad. I get it. "Glad to know you're proud of me, mom," I uttered in a sarcastic tone. Whoops! Where did that come from? Maybe she didn't hear me. I snuck a peak at my mom and was sorry I did. I was in even deeper trouble than a moment ago. Okay, time for a new strategy.

"It won't happen again, I promise," I said in a slightly louder, less sarcastic voice. I didn't specify if I meant getting up late or sassing my mom, but she seemed to buy the apology.

My dad, always the peacemaker, tried to smooth it over. "All we're saying Libby is even though this morning was not totally in your control, it just goes to show that being both the pet nanny and going to school is going to be difficult. I'm afraid we have to count this as Strike 1 of 3 in your *Pet Nanny Probation Period*. You have thirteen days left to prove you can do both."

I opened my mouth to share about the opportunity to join Debate Club and quickly shut it. I was kidding myself if they would ever entertain the idea. If anything, it would guarantee that I was

taking on too much. I sighed at the sacrifice of giving up Debate Club for the good of my Pet Nanny business.

Both my parents left to return to work, and I left to find George and thank him for covering for me. Maybe he had some idea of what I could do to make the business work. George always knew what to do. But I couldn't find George, so I decided to go see my best cat friend, Einstein. Then I remembered I no longer had Einstein's key. His mother had fired me. Maybe I could visit Rocky, my best dog friend. But then I remembered he and his parents would be moving in a few days, and now would not be a good time to interrupt the family. Instead, I cleaned up from lunch and went down to my Girl Cave. I was careful to stay awake and read my book so that I could do my afternoon check-in with Felix and Charley. I couldn't afford any more mistakes today.

CHAPTER 15

Probation Week 1 Successful!

Tuesday through Thursday at school and home were routine. Get up at 5:30. Get ready for school. Take Blaze et al. out for a walk and morning poop and return them home to their mother Anita without waking her. Feed and care for Felix and Charley. And starting on Thursday through Sunday take care of Odin, a fat Norwegian Forest cat both morning and night while its mother Maddie visited her out-of-state boyfriend. Then leave for school at 6:45. Go to class, try not to fall asleep during lessons and check in on Henry mid-morning. Then at night, it was just Odin and Felix and Charley requiring my attention, and that never took long because none of these cats required or desired much attention. Whew! I reminded myself how much rode on my remembering all these tasks and completing them successfully. I did not want to lose my Pet Nanny business.

On Tuesday Ms. Hart reminded the class that our Hero presentations would be this Friday and Inventor presentations next Friday. She asked for a show of hands of how many people had started researching their assignment. It seemed like most of the class raised their hands.

Then Ms. Hart said, continue to keep your hand up if you have finished your assignment. Only a few people kept their hands up. Whew, that was more like it. I didn't feel as panicky as I did a moment ago. Then I noticed one of the hands was waving in the air

as if to stay, "Look at me! Look at me!" It was Suzy Smarty Pants. Did I mention I don't like her? At all?

I pledged that I would start on my assignment immediately when I got home that afternoon. I was just thinking maybe my dad could drop me at the library that afternoon when Ms. Hart stopped by my desk and asked if I would please accompany her into the hall. Oh, no! Did I do something wrong? What is wrong with me?!! As soon as we were out in the hall Ms. Hart said, "Let's go take care of your kitty. We can talk in the vice principal's office."

Henry the cat was interested in the new human that entered his lair and plopped on her lap. Ms. Hart got to the point right away while petting Henry as if it was the most natural thing in the world to do. "Libby, I was surprised that you have not yet begun your assignment. Is there a reason why?"

I hesitated to answer honestly but I didn't want to lie to Ms. Hart either. I decided to come clean with her and hope that she didn't judge me. "You see, Ms. Hart, I have this pet sitting business called The Pet Nanny, and last weekend I was busy all weekend taking care of a dog and then yesterday I got a late start because I overslept and my parents said maybe I have to give up the business if I can't do both the business and school." I took a breath. That was a run-on sentence if I ever uttered one.

Ms. Hart looked like she was mulling over my confession. "That is a conundrum," she said.

"A conundrum? Is that a kind of musical instrument?" I asked her. I had never heard that phrase. In the meantime, while we were talking Henry had gotten off Ms. Hart's lap and was circling in and out of my ankles and actually started nipping at me. "OUCH! Henry, stop that," but I know what he wanted. He simply wanted to be fed.

As Ms. Hart explained the meaning of conundrum I fed Henry. "A conundrum is a situation that seems hopeless, until, of course, you share it with your teacher!" Ms. Hart smiled.

"I'm not sure yet how I can help with the pet sitting commitment, but I can help at the school end of the issue. I just happened to have this book about Joan of Arc from my private library. You're welcome to review it and return it to me after your presentation. Ms. Hart pulled a book seemingly out of the air and handed it to me.

"I also suggest you go to St. Peter's in the Loop. Are you familiar with it?" Ms. Hart saw me shake my head "no". "That's okay it's in between here and State Street. You are familiar with State Street, right? The heart of downtown Chicago?" To that question I nodded an enthusiastic yes. My mom used to take me to State Street every Christmas season to see the store windows decorated.

"Anyway, St. Peter's has an extensive book and gift shop in its basement and the prices are very reasonable. Here, take this," Ms. Hart handed me what I knew was a Holy Card – a laminated 2 inch by 4 inch card of a picture and prayer of a saint. The one I held in my hand was of St. Joan of Arc.

"Thank you, Ms. Hart!" I hoped I showed how appreciative I was of her advice and gifts.

"You can thank me by going to the store today and getting yourself another book about Joan of Arc so that you can prepare for Friday."

"I will! I will! I'm so excited to start reading." She nodded and directed me to the door. As usual, Henry didn't look up from his food when we left and when we returned to the classroom everyone stopped talking immediately and seemed to look at us expectantly. I saw fear in Steve's face and realized he thought I was in trouble. That might be a good cover, I thought, so I put my head down and avoided eye contact with everyone else until I got to my desk, and buried my head into my Joan of Arc book. I think I might have missed History but that's okay. What is Joan of Arc but not history?

That day when my dad picked me up I asked him if he knew where St. Peter's Church was, and he said, "Sure thing! I stop in there sometimes just to say a prayer."

I was shocked. "You do? Does mom know?" I always thought the teasing between my parents on my dad acting like a Catholic was just that – teasing.

"Well, we never really talk about it but it's not like it's a secret. How 'bout you? What's up with you wanting to go to St. Peter's?" My dad was definitely curious.

"My teacher suggested I visit the bookstore there and get a book on Joan of Arc for my presentation Friday." I answered.

"You mean THIS Friday? Do I understand you are just beginning your assignment?" My father doesn't get angry very often, but he sounded like he was on the edge of angry right now.

"Yes, but I have plenty of time. Can we stop by there now on the way home?" I realized where we were when I asked. We were going into our parking garage at home.

"I tell you what. Given the time constraint, I will walk with you over there after lunch AFTER your mom goes back to work. I don't want to explain why I'm going to St. Peter's. Okay?" My dad was trying to be helpful, so I readily agreed.

After a lunch of macaroni and cheese (not my favorite), my dad and I walked a few blocks to St. Peter's. It was beautiful inside and out. My father led the way to the stairwell going downstairs as if he'd been to the bookstore before and while it was smaller than I thought (I had envisioned a religious version of Barnes and Noble) it was just right for what I needed. The clerk helped me find the section on Joan of Arc and even suggested which book would be best. We were in and out of there in a matter of minutes and I couldn't wait to get home to start my research.

However, on the way out I stopped to look at the bulletin board. And so did my dad. He seemed to be reading a poster entitled "Why Not Tie the Knot Again?" I wasn't sure what that meant. Was it for boy scouts or sailors who needed to know how to tie knots better? My eyes had gone to the poster with pictures of dogs and cats and was that a bird? It read, "Join Us on October 4th for St. Francis Feast Day and the Annual Blessing of the Animals". Both posters were designed so you could simply pull off a copy of the 8 inches by 11 inches poster and take it home. Both my dad and I ripped off our posters at the same time, and for the first time in a few days we smiled and laughed together.

Dad asked if I could find my way home so that he could go straight to work, and I assured him I could get home safely on my own. He turned south and I turned west, and a block later there was George coming out of Walgreen's. He acted surprised to see me, but

I knew, somehow, he knew I'd be walking this way and I would be alone needing a guide back home.

George asked, "Going my way?"

"I am if you mean home, I replied.

"Here, this is for you," George handed me the bag he was carrying when he left Walgreens.

"What's this?" I asked while opening the bag, pulling out an alarm clock.

"That's a battery-operated alarm clock. Sorry they didn't have a Hello Kitty version, but at least it's pink, right?" George seemed disappointed over his choices of the clock, but I was thrilled to have a battery-operated alarm clock so I wouldn't over sleep ever again.

"Thanks George. It's an answer to a prayer," I said. George smiled and for once didn't disappear after performing one of his many heroic and unexpected acts of kindness.

"Hey, what do you have in the other bag?" George asked.

"It's a book on Joan of Arc," I said showing him the cover.

"Oh, that's right. Jerry told me you have to do a presentation on her for your Heroine assignment," George replied. I wondered for a moment how Jerry knew but then I stopped myself. George AND Jerry know all.

"I had an idea, Libby," George said. "You should dress up as Joan of Arc for your presentation. I happen to have the fixings for a Joan of Arc costume, if you're interested."

"Wow, George! That would be great! Do you think we can get it all together by Friday?" I asked, hoping the answer would be yes.

"I think so but remember. We can't spend too much time on it. You're on Pet Nanny Probation and the pets and your schoolwork have to come first." George reminded me.

"Gottcha! I think I can do it all," I said with just a little reservation in my voice. I felt like the little train that chanted "I think I can. I think I can. I think I can."

Well, it ended up I COULD do it all. With the help of Ms. Hart's book and prayer card and the book from St. Peter's bookstore I wrote my presentation without a problem. It kept the other kids' attention because Joan of Arc, patron saint of France, was our age

when she started hearing voices and receiving visions from deceased saints. The saints told her about her mission to help save France. My costume helped the kids visualize how Joan of Arc looked as a mighty warrior for France and for God. There was only one problem – Jerry made me give up my sword and held it until the end of the day. He was concerned with some weapon restrictions rule imposed by the school. Whatever. But because of the sword Ms. Hart warned future presenters that not only were costumes not necessary, they were not allowed. Too bad because mine was a big hit!

Despite the extra work of the Joan of Arc presentation, Week one of Pet Nanny Probation passed without incident. The weekend was easy enough because I had plenty of time to take care of the pets and no extra classwork to do. I only had 5 more class days to get through and Probation was over.

I couldn't wait for this next week to pass.

CHAPTER 16

Pet Probation Countdown

I set my new pink alarm from George extra early on Sunday night to make sure I could get everything done I needed to do before school Monday morning. Taking out Anita's trio was no problem, and I had no cats to look in on because all their parents were in town for the week, or at least until next Saturday when my probation would hopefully be lifted.

I even had time to run to Dunkin' Donuts and pick up donuts and coffee for my parents. Okay, and maybe a few donuts for me, too. They were pleasantly surprised, and maybe a little suspicious of my motives, but that was okay. Always keep them wondering. That's my motto.

School was uneventful. I got some more feedback on my Joan of Arc presentation. I especially liked that Steve thought I gave the best presentation so far. At least until it was his turn on Friday to present Thomas Alva Edison, inventor extraordinaire. He even took Saturday off from bird watching to prepare his paper and speech. I let him know my father missed his company, but that he respected Steve's sacrifice in the name of higher learning. My dad does come out with some pretty dorky sayings. Actually both my mom and dad do. It must be a parent thing.

I was happy to see that I got perfect scores in all my subjects both last week and this week. I was mostly glad because it was more evidence that I could do the pet sitting and excel at school.

Finally, Friday came, and it was time for Steve's presentation and it was GREAT! He didn't wear a costume, except for the hat I gave him that morning. It was a cap with a light bulb on top. I thought it was a great tribute to one of Edison's biggest inventions. Ms. Hart was less impressed and amended the No Costume Rule to include No Caps. And that was before she realized it could have been worse. Steve had deactivated the switch which allowed the cap to randomly light up. Thankfully the cap did not detract from Steve's grade as he parlayed it into part of his presentation when he noted that Edison did not invent the light bulb. Joseph Swan did, but Edison did produce the first commercially viable one. Even though Steve was obviously nervous, he gave his speech confidently and the whole class learned a lot about Edison, the Father of Invention and our school's namesake. Like my presentation on Joan of Arc the week before, Steve's presentation got an A Plus and we were the only two in the class to get A Plusses on our Hero and Inventor assignments.

I know what you're thinking. You're wondering how Suzy Smarty Pants did. Her presentation was on Henry Ford, inventor of the car. Except Ms. Hart pointed out at the end of Suzy's presentation that Henry Ford did not invent the car. He invented the moving assembly line making it easier to produce cars. And just like Suzy did with her speech to the class introducing herself where she had a handout to everyone (in the case of the first day it was Smarties candies), Suzy gave out little Hot Wheel cars to everyone. Except they were various models – not just Fords – so they were really not relevant. Ms. Hart must have agreed with my analysis because she outlawed presentation "give-aways" from that point forward. Good thing I rethought handing out French fries for my Joan of Arc speech!

CHAPTER 17

Adios Probation And Rocky

You guessed it! I passed Pet Nanny Probation. At least I assumed I did. Two weeks had passed, and nothing was said one way or another. The only strike against me was the first day of probation when the electricity went out overnight and I woke up late and George had to step in and help with the pets. I never really felt that should be a strike because the electricity going out was an act of God, or at least of the utility company, but since the lightening strike was my only strike, I could live with it. I MUST have passed probation.

The question now was: where do we go from here? And my parents had an answer for that question. "Libby," my mom called from the living room on Saturday afternoon. "Can you come here?"

My dad had just returned from bird watching and I was slow to leave my room. What if my parents had strikes up their sleeve? What if they changed the rules? I said a silent prayer to Joan of Arc to give me strength and approached the living room where my parents were sitting next to each other on the couch.

"What's up?" I asked, for lack of anything else to say.

My father started. "Steve said to say hi. He really wished you would like to join us for bird watching. I told him I'd try to convince you, but I also told him you are pretty busy with your pet sitting. By the way, how did it go today with the pets?"

Aahhh. Here we go. The verdict was in. And the envelope please?

I answered, "It went great. Anita gave me the weekend off and the four cats were no problem." I looked at them waiting for the announcement that Pet Nanny Probation was over. End of discussion.

My mom scooted forward and winced. Well, that didn't bode well. "Libby, we are very proud of how you handled the last two weeks and are happy to tell you that your probation period is over."

Whew! Crisis averted. I was about to make my escape when my mom kept on talking. Nooooooooo! No more need to keep on talking mom. I heard all I needed to hear.

"I have some good news. Your dad and I both have new clients for you. You remember last weekend when new people were moving into the building? One of our new neighbors is a co-worker of mine, and she has a schnoodle. Its name is Hans."

My heart dropped. How could I handle another dog to walk in addition to Anita's three dogs, especially in the morning. I was about to point out the obvious when I refocused on what my mom was saying. "My coworker Annmarie works the second shift so she wouldn't need you to walk Hans in the morning because she will be home then. Her hours are 3 p.m. to 9 p.m. so she would need you to take him out at 6-ish in the evening." Mom waited for my reaction.

"That actually could work. Thanks mom for scoring us a new client! When can I meet Annmarie and Hans?" I looked at my Hello Kitty watch to check the time. Why did it feel like I was forgetting something? I wondered.

My mom also checked her watch before saying we could check with Annmarie tomorrow, on Sunday, and visit at her convenience. And again I felt this mental twinge that I was forgetting something.

I looked at my dad and asked about his new client find. He looked so proud as he shared that he also had a co-worker with a dog. Again, my heart sunk. There was no way I could add a dog that needed to be walked in the morning.

But obviously dad had thought this through because he continued, "Bob bought a fixer upper in Indiana at Beverly Shores and has been dedicating his weekends to work on his new place. But he doesn't feel comfortable keeping his Havanese, Houdini, with him on the job site. He says it is just too dangerous (the job site, not Houdini). So he's looking for someone to take care of the dog on the weekend at their own home. He doesn't live too far away in Evanston. He'd drop the dog off on the way south to Indiana on Friday after work and then pick it up on Sunday early evening. The best part is since he is doing most of the work himself this could be a long-term arrangement."

My first reactions were #1 what the heck is a Havanese? And #2 what about when Rocky is staying with us. And then it came to me.... What I was forgetting. Rocky! Rocky and Carl and Kara were moving today. Rocky wouldn't be staying with us ever again. Sadness and panic intermixed as I tried to casually look at my watch. I couldn't let my parents realize that I had forgotten about Rocky's moving day. I had an inspiration.

"Hey mom and dad, that's great news on both fronts, but did you forget? Today is Rocky's moving day. Don't you think we better hurry upstairs and say our goodbyes?" Both my mom and dad looked embarrassed that the move slipped their minds. And I had smoothly escaped them realizing that it had also slipped mine. We quickly grabbed the goody bag we had made up over the past week with road trip treats for both canine and human alike and brought them to the seventh floor. Rocky heard (smelled?) us coming and was barking when we got off the elevator. As his father opened the door, he jumped on each of us in turn, wagging the whole time. I don't remember much else except for the tears. There were lots of tears. And I remembered George standing in the hallway with a box of Kleenex. And before he handed over the box he took a couple for himself. I think we could all agree there would never be another dog like Rocky. I sure will miss that dog.

CHAPTER 18

Fall Begins

I woke up on Sunday in a puddle of tears and wondered if we had a roof leak when I realized why my pillowcase was wet. I remembered that Rocky and his family had started their long move to Seattle yesterday and I almost started crying again. Until I remembered, there were lots of happy reasons to get up today. First off my parents promised a special Sunday breakfast in Chicago. We were going to Lou Mitchell's, a Chicago diner that had been around for almost a hundred years. My dad said that there was always a long line but that while you stood in it the hostess handed out donut holes and Milk Duds. I couldn't wait.

I got up and quickly dressed happily anticipating going to a new restaurant. My parents were on the couch holding hands and seemed oblivious to my approach. And then I saw my mom was crying. Oh, no. What did my dad say to her? Poor mommy. I hope they weren't considering divorce again. But then my mom turned and I saw she was smiling and looking at her hand. What was that glare? Was that the sunshine reflecting on something? Wait a minute.... Was that a new ring on my mom's hand?

"What's going on?" I demanded. My parents laughed at my confusion.

My dad spoke up first. "I asked your mom to marry me again, and she said YES!" They both looked so happy. I glanced at the new ring. It was HUGE!

"I don't get it. You're already married and your divorce didn't happen so why would you do it again?" And then I thought about it and it occurred to me that I always wanted to be a flower girl, but no one ever asked me. I was too old to be a flower girl but maybe this time I could be a bridesmaid. Oh, I hope mom will let me get a blue dress. While pink is my favorite color, I think for a bridesmaid, I'd rather wear blue and then I could be mom's something blue! You know, as in, something borrowed, something blue, something old, something new.

"Can I be your bridesmaid? Can I wear a blue formal flowing dress with flowers in my hair?" I pleaded.

My parents laughed at me. Again. My dad said, "It isn't that kind of ceremony. It's a short ceremony where a group of couples exchange their vows during a special mass at St. Peter's. They call it "Tie the Knot Again." And then I remembered the poster that dad took the day we went to the church for my Joan of Arc book.

"Oh. Well, that's a disappointment. I mean, not about the wedding, but about not getting to be a bridesmaid. Can I come too?"

Without hesitation my parents said in unison, "Absolutely!"

"It's next Sunday after the St. Francis Feast Day Blessing of the Animals," my dad added. And then I had a memory flash. I remembered taking a poster from the bulletin board when my dad had taken the "Tie the Knot Again Poster." I went to fetch it from my room and saw that the St. Francis Blessing was next Sunday like my dad said.

"Can we go early and see what the St. Francis Feast Day Blessing is all about?" I asked. And my parents readily agreed on the condition that I would keep smiling like I was at that moment for the rest of the day.

It wasn't hard to keep smiling. Lou Mitchell's was delicious, especially the donut holes and milk duds. And in the afternoon I got to meet my two new dog clients: Hans the schnoodle and his mother Annmarie, and Houdini, the Havanese, and his father Bob. Due to a miscommunication between my mom and dad, everyone showed up at the same time and everyone braced themselves for a dog fight.

But Houdini and Hans wagged and playfully pulled at their leashes anxious to greet their new best canine friend.

And call me crazy but there seemed to be something between Annmarie and Bob, too. I mentioned it to my mom after everyone left, and she said, "Since when have you become such a romantic? Oh, wait a minute, since *Steve* maybe?" I didn't like the way she emphasized *Steve*.

"Forget it, mom. You're right. Nothing going on there. They probably just had gas." I slunk back to my room and stopped smiling despite my promise to keep smiling for the rest of the day. I wish Mom would stop teasing me about Steve.

Monday morning dawned quickly and I was anxious to get to school. We were going to pick our new topics for the whole month of October. As promised, when we entered our classroom, there were orange and black balloons. I couldn't wait for the announcement of what the new topics were.

Ms. Hart rang her trio of morning bells, called roll call, and then added a children's bugle call to her repertoire to announce the presentation topics for October. Her voice rang out from the front of the classroom, "Next Friday we will start our October presentations and instead of ten minutes, these will be twenty minutes and I expect you to include physical specimens representing your topic. These specimens can include posters, pictures, diagrams, smaller items, etc., but nothing living or breathing. And a reminder: No costumes! No caps or hats! Because your presentations will be longer than the ones this month we should be able to spread them over the whole month."

Ms. Hart hesitated and then asked, "What does October remind you of?" And almost everyone in the class answered "HALLOWEEN!"

'And what does Halloween remind you of?" This time several people raised their hand to answer. Ms. Hart called on each of them in turn. One answered, "Trick or Treat." Another answered, "Costumes." A third said "Witches and devils." The fourth said "Mysteries", and Ms. Hart clapped her hands at that response. She explained that in honor of Halloween the two topics would be "Mysteries" as depicted by the orange balloons, and "Scary stuff" topics which would be found in the black balloons.

Steve and I agreed that we were uncertain of what topics would be found in the balloons and which one we would prefer to pop, but Ms. Hart explained that there would be no choice to make. She would be calling out our names alphabetically in reverse order and then each person would pop a balloon starting with black and then the next person would pop an orange balloon, then black, then orange, etc. I wonder what Ms. Hart does for fun because she spends way too much time thinking up these assignments!

Ms. Hart looked at me and said, "Before we start popping, Libby, why don't you go warn our vice principal that we will be making unconventional noises so we don't disturb him." I got the hint that not only was I to deliver the message but I was also supposed to take care of Henry.

I happily went down the hall to Jerry's office and Henry was waiting patiently for me on the other side of Jerry's office door. I closed the door and bent down to pet Henry. I noticed that in the past month Henry had grown. In fact, technically he was no longer a kitten. Nor was he a full grown cat. He was a teenager, just like me! Well, maybe not just like me. He wasn't as moody! I made quick work of petting and feeding Henry because I was anxious to pick my October assignment contained in the orange and black balloons.

Ms. Hart addressed the class. "Any guesses what topics are in the balloons?" I heard a lot of guesses as I left the room and took care of my tasks. When I returned, Ms. Hart said, "I tell you what. Since Friday is only four days away, the first five people who volunteer to present this Friday can spend the rest of the class period in the library to get a head start on their topic."

My hand shot up before anyone else, followed by Steve's, two others behind us, and, you guessed it, Suzy Smarty Pants. Arghhh. I wonder if her name was listed as a topic in the Scary Things balloons. The five of us formed a line. Somehow Suzy wiggled up in second position behind Steve. Steve popped a black balloon, Suzy an orange, and in last position, I got to pop a black balloon. Steve waited for me to pick up my topic off the floor before he looked at his piece of paper. Suzy was cooing over her orange mystery slip of paper but we both ignored her and went by the world map posted on the side wall.

I thought it was just to get away from Suzy but it was because Steve wanted to look at the map.

"Look. My scary topic is Dracula," Steve said. "I wanted to see where Transylvania is on the map." It took us a few minutes to find it as Transylvania is a very small country located in central Europe. "Oh, look – now it's Romania," Steve noticed.

"I think you get the pick of the draw by picking THE vampire. I don't even know who my scary topic is," I confessed to Steve.

"Well, what is it?" Steve asked.

I jumped when Suzy snuck up on us and asked, "Yeh, Libby, what's your topic? I'm sure Steve and I will know who or what it is," Suzy said smugly.

"Well, you know, Suzy, I'd like to share but that would ruin the surprise on Friday," I said snippily. I turned to Steve and said, "I'm off to the library. Wanna come?"

Steve put his right arm up against the lower portion of his face and in his best attempt at a Dracula imitation said, "I vant to go to the library with you Meez Libby." We both laughed and left before Suzy could invite herself.

CHAPTER 19

A Busy October

October started out with a bang. On the first Friday of October the "scary stuff" and "mystery" presentations began. Steve's topic, Dracula the vampire, was a big hit as was his false fangs and mini-coffin. He also walked over to the wall map on the side of the classroom and pointed out where Transylvania was. He used a Dracula accent and if you closed your eyes you could imagine it was Dracula himself doing the presentation uttering the classic line, "I vant to suck your blood," at the end of his talk.

Suzy Smarty Pants had picked a "mystery" topic and her talk was about the Egyptian pyramids. I hate to admit it, but the topic was intriguing. It truly is impressive that the pyramids were constructed with over 2 million bricks weighing several tons each in an era when there was no heavy construction machinery. Her physical specimens were a miniature pyramid, and a "papyrus" scroll for each of us in the class. It was only a rolled-up piece of paper, but we were to pretend it was Egyptian papyrus. Our names were written on tags on each scroll. As each classmate unrolled it there were oohs and aahs. Suzy had gone to the Field Museum in Chicago where there is a huge Egyptian exhibit. I went there a few years back on a field trip with my old school. There is a display with an oversized laptop and a slot where you can insert your credit card. In exchange for a charge on your parent's credit card you can type in a name and a piece of paper will print out the name in hieroglyphics. Even Ms. Hart got a scroll with her name in hieroglyphics, which is probably why she didn't remind

the class of the "no give-aways" rule. Adding insult to injury was the probability that Suzy Smarty Pants would surely get an A Plus!

I was the last person on the assignment roster that Friday to present my "scary" topic. The other presentations were great and tough acts to follow. When I first pricked the black balloon and carefully unfolded the slip of paper that fell out, I was confused. I had never heard of "Sasquatch". I couldn't wait to research it and when I saw my first photo of "Sasquatch" I knew exactly who it was. Well, that's not true. No one truly knows who he or it is, or whether it even exists. Which is why I pointed out to Ms. Hart and the class that the existence of Sasquatch is both a mystery and a scary creature. People who claim to have seen him describe him as a large and scary half man/half animal. Because of his hugeness, some call him Bigfoot. He allegedly lives in the extreme northern parts of North America. When I was researching him I wondered if the Wisconsin Dells qualified as Bigfoot territory. As I was ending my presentation, I jumped as I felt a hand on my shoulder. I hadn't noticed someone come in the class door behind me. I looked behind me and there was Bigfoot in the flesh! The whole class laughed as I screamed. I didn't need my physical specimens, a cardboard cutout of what I imagined was Sasquatch's big foot covered in multi-colored fur and photos of him smiling. Thanks to George, who dressed up as Bigfoot, I had the real thing. And like she did with Suzy, Ms. Hart overlooked the "no living thing" rule.

After my presentation I accompanied George/Bigfoot back to his brother Jerry's office to introduce him to Henry the cat. Henry took to George right away and George commented, "I thought you said this was a kitten. This is a full grown cat, Libby!" Henry looked at George with appreciation for his compliment. I looked at Henry through George's eyes and saw him in a new light. Maybe I'd been feeding him too much! And I realized something else. If I did feed him too much it was because I loved Henry so much and wanted to spend more time with him. Jerry was lucky to have Henry as a pet.

Luckily that weekend I had no pet sitting duties. I was relieved because I had fallen a little behind in my homework and needed the time to catch up. On Saturday, as always, my dad and Steve invited me to join them on their birdwatching walk. I begged off to study. I wouldn't be able to study on Sunday because my parents were renewing their wedding vows and we all planned to attend the St. Francis Blessing of Animals beforehand. It ended up Aunt Lori joined us early Sunday morning and we all walked the half mile to St. Peter's Church in the middle of the Chicago loop. I asked my dad if he knew why they called it a loop and he explained that the loop referred to the elevated train that forms a loop around the area of skyscrapers and other attractions. I asked if we lived in the loop and he said we didn't. I was a little disappointed to be left out of the loop.

When we arrived at St. Peter's there was a crowd of people on the stairs of the church. Each person held a pet or tugged on a leash tied to a pet. There were howls and meows and multiple human voices urging their animal to keep quiet. But what was amazing was that none of the animals seemed aggressive. They were just being cats and dogs. We got there right at the start. A priest was asking everyone to form a circle up and down the stairs, with the priest in the middle. He welcomed everyone and gave a short speech of who St. Francis was and how important animals were to the saint. He said a prayer for the animals and then proceeded to walk around the circle. He carried with him what I assumed was a bottle of holy water, which he sprinkled on each animal as he muttered a blessing. Every animal was speechless during this time as if they were under the priest's spell. When the priest came to my family he asked where our animal was. I replied, "Good question," and looked accusingly at my parents. The priest moved on and my parents decided it was time to go into the church and get good seats for their second wedding.

The same priest came in about a half an hour later and greeted the dozen couples and their families that had come to renew their wedding vows. The priest explained the concept of tying the knot a second time and congratulated every couple present for their continued love and commitment to each other. At one point he asked each couple to stand and face each other while holding hands. I had taken the whole pew in front of them in protest for not having a pet of my own and for the first time saw my mom in profile. Poor mom. She had gained weight! No more McDonalds for her. But I wouldn't say anything today and ruin my parent's special day.

The ceremony was short. I imagine it was much shorter than their original wedding. The priest said a final blessing and a final song played as the recessional hymn. I was familiar with it – it was the song Turn! Turn! Turn! by the Byrds. It was one of my parent's favorite songs. And for the first time I really listened to the lyrics:

To everything turn, turn, turn
There is a season turn, turn, turn
And a time to every purpose under Heaven

A time to be born, a time to die
A time to plant, a time to reap
A time to kill, a time to heal
A time to laugh, a time to weep

To everything turn, turn, turn
There is a season turn, turn, turn
And a time to every purpose under Heaven

A time to build up, a time to break down
A time to dance, a time to mourn
A time to cast away stones
A time to gather stones together

To everything turn, turn, turn
There is a season turn, turn, turn
And a time to every purpose under Heaven

A time of love, a time of hate
A time of war, a time of peace
A time you may embrace
A time to refrain from embracing

To everything turn, turn, turn
There is a season turn, turn, turn
And a time to every purpose under Heaven

A time to gain, a time to lose
A time to rain, a time to sow
A time for love, a time for hate
A time for peace, I swear it's not too late

And I thought to myself.... And a time to renew your wedding vows AND a time to get a dog!

Afterward my dad surprised us with a special meal at Gibson's on the Chicago River. I was surprised that I never noticed it before as it was very close to our apartment. I asked my dad at the end of the delicious meal if we could come here every Sunday. He asked if I had a trust fund that he didn't know about. Sometimes he speaks in riddles but I guess that was a "no".

CHAPTER 20

Fall Begins

With the addition of my two new doggy clients, Hans and Houdini, it was time to pay more attention to the Pet Nanny business. I was facing the same dilemma that I had at the beginning of the school season: how to balance school and pet sitting? I didn't want my parents to give me any more ultimatums about quitting the Pet Nanny business.

It was Saturday and it was my first weekend caring for Houdini at our house. For a small dog, he was incredibly strong. He pulled hard at his leash and as we reached the sidewalk outside the front door of the building, I stumbled straight into a stranger waiting on the other side of the door.

Ouch! "I am so sorry," I said apologetically to the young man smiling down at Houdini.

"Look, mom! It's a Havanese!," the stranger said to a woman standing next to him. There was something about his voice that didn't match his height or age, which I guessed was at least ten years older than me.

The woman went to pet Houdini but before she could, the dog jumped up on her, tail wagging. Now it was time to apologize to her. "I'm so sorry," I repeated. "Evidently Houdini is not in an obedient mood today. I hope he didn't get your skirt dirty."

The woman smiled and said, "No worries. Both my son and I love dogs. Do you live in this building?"

"I do with my parents, but not with Houdini. I am just pet-sitting him." I was curious why she asked, but she quickly explained.

"My son and I are looking at an apartment in this building. We are supposed to meet...." But before she could complete her sentence, George appeared and finished her sentence. "George – and here I am! Let me show you and your son your new apartment."

The woman looked puzzled. "Oh, we are here to look but we haven't made any decisions yet," she told George. George looked at me, then back at the lady, and smiled. "I have your key right here!" Two weeks later it didn't surprise me one bit when the woman and her son moved in our building.

Houdini's stay at our house was uneventful, and on Sunday night I was sad to see him leave. We found out why he was named Houdini. It was after the famous magician in the early 1900's who was an escape artist. Bob, Houdini's owner, explained that when the dog was younger, he too was an escape artist, and could wiggle out of any harness or collar within moments of it being put on. Thankfully, he was past this stage and was now relatively well behaved.

Once Houdini left, our pizza from Giordano's arrived. It was a deep dish meat special – sausage, bacon, pepperoni and ham. My dad and I dug in immediately, but my mom quickly excused herself and escaped down the hall. One Houdini left, and another disappeared, just like that! My dad didn't seem concerned, but I could hear muffled sounds from the bathroom, like maybe my mom was throwing up.

"Dad, I think mom is sick," I said.

"How's that?" he asked, reaching for a second slice of pizza.

"I think mom is throwing up. Should you go see if she's okay?" I asked, carefully not volunteering for what could be a messy job.

"Aww, Sweetie, she's okay. It's just..." he stopped abruptly.

"Just what?" I asked, alarm in my voice.

"Just what?" my mom asked, having suddenly appeared behind me.

"Libby was just asking why you were throwing up down the hall." My dad said looking pointedly at my mom.

"Oh, that. I just found out the smell of bacon makes me sick! Go figure! But don't worry, I'll just take the bacon off my share of the pizza." My mom reached for her first piece of pizza and that was the end of the conversation. Except I kept thinking about it. If my mom thought the bacon smelled funny, I was thinking the same thing about my mom's explanation. But before I could dwell on it, I realized the pizza was disappearing quickly. I had to take my share before the pizza did a "Houdini."

CHAPTER 21

Halloween

The next day at school Ms. Hart made an announcement about Halloween, which was only a few weeks away. "Class – attention please. As you know Halloween is on Friday, October 31st. While the school prohibits costumes (even ones of famous saints like Joan of Arc), I would like to offer you the opportunity to participate in a costume contest. By Monday, October 27th, please bring a photo of you in a costume. It can be a new costume, or one from a few years back. I will make up a ballot and distribute it on Halloween. Obviously, the one who gets the most votes, wins! Any questions?"

Ralph, the boy who sat behind me, raised his hand. "Yes. I have a question. What's the prize?"

While I was curious as well, it seemed rude of Ralph to ask. But Ms. Hart didn't seem offended. "Well, Ralph, what do you think an appropriate prize would be on *Trick or Treat* day?"

"Candy!" Ralph shouted with a big smile.

"Well, that's a thought," Ms. Hart said as if it had never occurred to her to give out candy on Halloween. "I'll certainly consider it," she said with a knowing smile of her own.

Every one of my classmates had the same goal: to win their weight in candy on Halloween.

After class, I approached Steve. "Hey, you're good on the computer, right?"

Steve said tentatively, "Yes. What do you need, Libby?"

"Who said I need anything? I was just trying to give you a compliment." I said defensively.

"Whatever it is, I'm happy to help you," Steve said.

"Well, as long as you don't mind, here's what I'm thinking. Ms. Hart gave me the idea of having a pet costume contest in my building. But I need your help with the computer end of it. I'm thinking I'd have the pet owners send me a picture of their pet in a costume by email and then I'd print out the pictures on my apartment door and number them, one through ten, or however many contestants there are. I'd ask people to email me their vote for favorite animal costume by Halloween eve, and then announce the winner by return email and on the apartment door as well." I hadn't really thought any of this out, but as I said it out loud, it seemed doable.

"Libby, you better prohibit people from voting for their own pet. Otherwise, you'll have a ten or twenty-way tie," Steve offered.

Of course, he was right. He was always right. *He's so smart*, I thought.

"What?" I asked as I realized Steve had asked something as I slipped into a daydream.

"What will you give as a prize? Pet treats?" Steve suggested.

"Nope. This is a business promotion. They'll get a 10% discount on their next visit by the Pet Nanny," I announced.

"Okay," Steve said. "But I think if I were a dog, I'd rather have a bone."

"Point taken. So it's a good thing the pets can't read the contest rules," I pointed out.

Two weeks later, both costume contests – at work and home – went well. My photo as Joan of Arc did not win. Ralph's costume photo was of him in the winning costume of a "MOG" (half man-half dog) from the movie Space Balls, which his mother had made last year. None of us had ever heard of the movie or of a "MOG" but the costume was definitely superior to the rest of our costume photos, most of which were bought from the store.

The pet costume contest at home was fun, and I enjoyed looking at my email at night to see if there were any new contestants. The night before Halloween I chose a winner: a cat dressed up as a multi-colored caterpillar. Like Ralph, her cat mom made her costume. The best part is Chloe, the cat, was my newest client. Her mom, Cecelia, explained that she wouldn't need me very frequently, but she'd be happy to cash in on her 10% Pet Nanny discount the next time she was out of town.

That night I realized that no one had knocked at the door or yelled out Trick or Treat. I missed my house in the suburbs where Trick or Treaters lined up and down the sidewalk waiting for a piece of candy. But I also realized it was the end of the month, and my parents hadn't complained once about my missing schoolwork because of my pet sitting. AND I gained three new clients during the month. It was a good month after all. And the best part? My mom didn't know whether we would have trick or treaters and bought a huge bag of candy. Someone had to eat it!

Steve's parents said he could stay that evening since it was not a school night, and my dad streamed a Halloween movie for us to watch: Ghostbusters! And Steve was quick to point out that the movie was rated PG-13. It was my first PG-13 movie and I got to watch it with Steve sitting next to me on the couch. Well, at least until my parents joined us and encouraged Steve to sit in the recliner. We had pizza and popcorn and trick-or-treat candy. It was probably a perfect night, but I can't be sure. I fell asleep midway through the movie!

CHAPTER 22

First Monday Of November

The first Monday of November Ms. Hart was full of announcements regarding November assignments and activities. But notably missing were balloons at the entrance of the classroom. I wondered if Ms. Hart had forgotten our November assignments.

And then I noticed the writing on the wall. Well, actually, the writing on the board in the front of the classroom. It read:

ELECTION OF 1860

ABRAHAM LINCOLN V. STEPHEN DOUGLAS V. JOHN BELL V. JOHN BRECKINRIDGE

Before I could puzzle any further, Ms. Hart rang her succession of now familiar bells and we clamored for our seats. I leaned over and said to Steve, "What's with the board – I think Ms. Hart lost 150 years, right?" Steve grinned and shrugged his shoulders.

"I'll tell you *all* what's with the election announcement, Libby," Ms. Hart declared in a voice loud enough for the class to hear. I jumped in my seat not knowing that she had been standing there.

Ms. Hart addressed the class. "November is a short month as school is closed the week of Thanksgiving." Before she could speak further, the classroom broke out in a huge round of hurrays and applause at the prospect of having a week off.

Ms. Hart responded with, "I'm glad you are all appreciative of this rare opportunity to be off school." I couldn't tell if she was sincere or sarcastic. It didn't matter. I *was* unapologetically looking forward to a week without assignments. But I would miss Steve. I might have to break my bird watching rule after all if I wanted to see him that week.

Ms. Hart continued. "Before I talk about the 1860 election, let me tell you what our daily November activity will be. Every day, including today, I will ask one of you to share with the class your personal "thankful" list. Before Thanksgiving each you will tell us what you are thankful for in the past, in the present, and in the future. I'll write your list down on the posterboard I placed over the map on the east wall so when we lose sight of our good fortunes, we can look over at the posterboard."

Ms. Hart looked at me. At some level I knew what was coming. "Libby," she said.

"Yes, Ms. Hart?" I answered avoiding her eyes. *Maybe she wants to remind me to take care of Henry. That's it.... I sighed with relief. I was so afraid she wanted me to declare my thankful list right here and now.*

And then, just as I was convinced I was off the hook, Ms. Hart did just that. "Libby, since you have proven in the past you are so good at "adlibbying", why don't you demonstrate how easy this assignment will be?" Ms. Hart motioned for me to stand up and she took up a position at the posterboard writing my name at the top in green marker.

I took a minute to think and said, "The thing I am grateful for in the past is that my parents were going to get a divorce and then changed their minds. They are together now. They even just got remarried! And the thing I am grateful for right now in the present is that I am able to do okay in school and still run my pet sitting business. But, Ms. Hart, how can I say what I'm grateful for in the future without it happening yet?" There was rumbling in the classroom as many of my other fellow students expressed the same confusion.

Ms. Hart explained. "Have you ever heard of visualization'?" She looked around the classroom to see if anyone would raise their hand.

When none of us did, she explained. "Visualization is when you come up with an idea of how you want something to happen and then take steps to make sure it does. It's sort of a wish. Libby, can you think of anything like that?" Ms. Hart asked.

And in a second I knew exactly what I would wish for and what one thing would make me more thankful than ever. "Yes, Ms. Hart. Write this down please: a new addition to my family." *Wait a minute! I wanted to say a new pet. Oh well, same difference. I mean, what else could 'new addition' mean?*

Ms. Hart raised her eyebrow. "I think that fate might have that in store for you and your family, Libby." She said it so convincingly that I had full confidence I was going to get the pet I wished for. I wondered if my parents had confided in her and whether she knew if it would be a cat or a dog.

Ms. Hart continued, "Class, I expect each of you to have your list of past, present and future thankful blessings ready because you'll never know what day I may call upon you." Spoiler alert: everyone made up a list of blessings that day and everyone was ready to share when called upon. Easiest assignment ever! Especially the future blessing – it was like wishing on a genie lamp!

"Now," Ms. Hart continued. "As many of you probably know, presidential elections are currently held every four years in November. To commemorate that process, we are going to revisit the 1860 election. I want each of you to write down the information on the board. I have scheduled library visits all this week for groups of five for an hour each. The librarian has already pulled all the available information on these four candidates that ran in the election. Each of you are to review information on the election itself and the four candidates and choose one candidate to write a short essay on, which I want you to turn in to me by Thursday. Of course, you are welcome to do outside research. On Friday bring in a copy of your short essay and any background research you did. Be prepared a rare opportunity: at the age of thirteen you are going to have the opportunity to vote!"

Ms. Hart was being rather cryptic and I didn't like the tight turnaround time for the assignment, but I knew I was going to write about Lincoln. Why pick a loser when you knew the winner in advance?

CHAPTER 23

First Weekend Of November

The first week of November went quickly and researching Lincoln specifically for his participation in 1860 proved to be more difficult than I thought. I turned in my "short" essay on Lincoln (if you consider 10 single space typed pages short) to Ms. Hart on Thursday and wondered what she was up to for the next day.

On Friday morning Ms. Hart congratulated all of us on our research and pointed out that she was surprised so many of us took the easy route and chose Lincoln as the candidate to research. I was embarrassed that Ms. Hart may think less of me. She reported that at least a few had chosen the other candidates so that her exercise could take place. She asked for a drum roll. We all obeyed and table drummed on our desks.

Ms. Hart motioned for us to quit drumming and announced, "Today we will recreate the 1860 Presidential Election, but first we will hold a short debate between the four candidates running for president. Based on your essays, I have selected four of you to serve as presidential candidates. Can I have Kenny come forward?"

Slowly Kenny creeped forward to the front of the room. I hadn't noticed that four podiums had been placed behind Ms. Hart. Kenny stepped behind the one labeled John Bell, and then asked if he needed his notes. Ms. Harat said, "Sorry. I should have told those of you called to bring your notes and essay copy with you." As Kenny went back for his notes, Ms. Hart called upon John W. (as opposed to John H. and John B.) to take the podium marked John

Breckinridge, followed by Joy to play the part of Stephen Douglas. I held my breath. I really was not up for playing Abraham Lincoln. Those were too big shoes to fill, and I was only a size 5. And then I saw Suzy Smarty Pants wearing a stovetop hat and standing behind the Lincoln podium. I instantly regretted not "visualizing" myself playing Lincoln. I knew I would have done him justice – at least better than Suzy ever could.

Ms. Hart asked each candidate in turn to recite their name, their party affiliation, and why, in one short sentence, they thought they should be elected. After that exercise she said she would act as moderator and ask each candidate a question and then allow the candidates to comment on the other candidates' platforms.

The debate took longer than I thought and was much more passionate than I predicted. At the end, Ms. Hart thanked each of the candidates for travelling so far in time to meet with her class and passed out ballots to each of us to select our favorite nominee. Each of the candidates received an A Plus for their participation, including Suzy Smarty Pants.

Lincoln won, of course, but the other candidates received an appreciable amount of votes as well. Suzy was way too smiley and took so many bows her hat fell off. I held my tongue. I wanted to remind her how she'd end up in a few years thanks to John Wilkes Booth.

Because of the election I was late taking care of Henry. He meowed loudly when I came in the door. I said it before and I'll say it again. Cats have internal clocks because they always know when I am late. "Shhhh," I warned Henry. I've kept his existence and my cat duties a secret this long. I didn't want to blow it now.

Henry quieted down and I probably spent longer than I should cuddling him before feeding him. By the time I got back to the classroom I noticed that Ms. Hart had hung a spectacular map on the wall with notations and drawings all over it. I was curious as a cat and went to look at it. I saw the caption at the top: Tribes of the Indian Nation. Obviously, this was created a long time ago because it should have used the term "Native American" Nation and not Indian. In any event it was amazing how many tribes were listed and I wondered why it was hung up for all to see.

Then I noticed the intricately woven basket on the desk full of envelopes and before I could see if they were labeled Ms. Hart cleared her throat and asked that everyone take their seats. I looked around and noticed everyone else *was* seated which meant she was talking to me.

"I can tell some of you are more curious than the others as to what is in this basket and if it has anything to do with the new map on the wall. The simple answer is, YES it does!" Ms. Hart exclaimed with enthusiasm.

"As you know, on the first Thanksgiving, the pilgrims invited the local native Americans to a dinner. This set the stage for peace between the new arrivals to this country and its native inhabitants. Unfortunately, peace between the two races did not last for long and as a result a nation that boasted hundreds of native American tribes now can only claim a few in comparison." Ms. Hart paused to see if her students understood the importance of this fact before continuing.

"To honor these true "founders" of our country your assignment, due next Friday, is to research a native American tribe. These envelopes in my authentic native American basket each contain the name of a native American tribe. As you leave today, please grab an envelope and over the next week prepare a report on that tribe. It doesn't need to be lengthy. Please keep your report to ten minutes or less." As Ms. Hart motioned to the basket, the bell rang. We all gathered our belongings and made sure to grab an envelope. Some people who shall not be named tried to look at the names on the envelopes and Ms. Hart was quick to reprimand Suzy (oops! I didn't mean to say who) that she was to *randomly* select her envelope. As Ms. Hart was speaking with Suzy, I took the opportunity to sneak a peek myself and picked the Winnebago Nation. I was happy to "pick" this tribe because I knew they were from my favorite vacation spot, Wisconsin Dells. I couldn't wait to start my assignment.

When I got home I quickly gobbled down lunch and afterwards glanced at the pet sitting calendar. WHAAAT? I internally screamed. The weekend was full. All of my regulars as well as my newest clients were going out of town and needed my help.

"Is something wrong?" I jumped at the sound of my mother's voice. I thought she had gone back to work.

"Nope. Everything is okie dokie." I wondered if she noted that my voice was about an octave higher than usual.

"Really," my mom said. "Because I would have thought you'd be a little concerned with how you are going to handle everything. And still get your native American assignment done." My mom seemed to be enjoying this moment at my expense.

"I'm going to map out the weekend right now. Were you thinking of volunteering to help?" I asked knowing the answer but half hoping she would pitch in.

"Nope. I'm sure everything will be okie dokie, just like you said." She turned to go to work but not before I caught the smirk. It was going to be a long weekend.

I ate dinner quickly and excused myself from the table. That evening was my first time to walk Hans, the schnoodle. Up until now Hans' mother, Annmarie, had been running home at 6 p.m. to take Hans out, but she finally decided that it was more prudent to just let me walk him. Before I went to Hans' apartment, I checked in on Charley and Felix, Kelly the stewardess' cats, and then quickly fed Odin and cleaned his litter box. His mother Maddie was visiting her boyfriend. Luckily, Chloe's mother, Cecelia, cancelled at the last minute. Whew! I needed to be home by 7 p.m. for Bob's arrival with Houdini who would be staying with us all weekend. I got home minutes before then and scanned my list to make sure I didn't forget anyone. I was glad to see I had checked everyone off the list.

Houdini sniffed his temporary territory and when he was convinced everything was to his satisfaction, he crawled into his bed that Bob had dropped off earlier. Houdini was happy with his bed as long as the humans were up and about. The minute I went to bed Houdini relocated to my bed. And that was okay with me. I missed Rocky doing the same thing.

My phone was ringing early the next morning. It was Anita. She had forgotten to tell me that she needed me to walk her three dogs Buddy, Brownie and Blaze, three times a day this weekend. She had a conference downtown and couldn't make it home during the day to take care of them. Luckily these extra hours were only over the weekend. I assured her I could handle it.

I got up quickly and dressed, all the while urging Houdini to get up as well. As soon as I put on my shoes, I slipped Houdini's collar and leash on and headed for the door. It would have to be a short walk because Anita's brood would be needing walking very soon. I didn't expect anyone else to be up this early and almost tripped over someone sitting on the front steps of the building.

"Oh, I'm sorry," I uttered as Houdini licked the face of the man sitting on the step. Wait, that wasn't a man – it was the new guy who moved in recently with his mother.

"Houdini, stop it. It's not polite to kiss strangers," I chastised Houdini. For some reason the new neighbor guy thought this was funny, and continued interacting with Houdini, much to his delight.

"Hey, we have to go but thank you for tolerating Houdini. He doesn't mean any harm," I said.

Strangely the guy looked sad as he merely nodded. He got up off the step and opened the door to the outside for us, but never said a word. Maybe he didn't remember us from the first day he and his mom visited the building. I didn't have time to think about it much until twenty minutes later when I took out Blaze, Brownie and Buddy. And the guy was still sitting there.

"Excuse me and the brood," I said in his direction as I tried to steer the dogs out of the door.

He looked up and smiled. "Good morning. Have I met you before?"

I took his comment to mean had we been formally introduced. I put out my hand and said, "Hi, I'm Libby. And you are?"

"Marcus. I just moved in the building with my mom. She snores in the morning," he shared.

"Well, snores happen, I guess. Would you mind getting the door again for me and the dogs?" I asked politely.

"Again?" he asked.

I was confused. Did he not remember me and Houdini being out here a few minutes ago? It didn't matter. I had a job to do. But before I could say 'never mind, I'll do it myself', he got up like a gentleman and opened the door. The dogs barreled through and we were off to the races. I thanked Marcus and when we got back, he was gone.

The day was filled with dogs and cats and I didn't have any time to ponder Marcus' behavior. Since it was a Saturday I didn't have to take out Hans as his mother was off on the weekend. I asked my mom if Houdini had barked when I took out Anita's dogs. She laughed. No, he was too tired to care where you were. And by the way, he snores. I had this sudden memory of Marcus sharing that his mother snored, and it made me wonder what his deal was.

"Hey, mom, I need to go see George before he leaves. I'll be right back." I didn't wait for permission and left quickly to find George.

Of course he was waiting right outside the door.

"Hey, George. I have a question. You know the new mother and son that moved in?" I prompted.

"Yes," George said hesitantly.

"Well, I ran into Marcus this morning and a few minutes later I saw him again and he acted like he never saw me before. Do you think he was sleepwalking?" I asked.

George was uncharacteristically quiet. "I tell you what Libby. Next time you see his mother Patti in the hall alone tell her you met Marcus and see what she is willing to share with you. It's not my place to say anything."

Now it was really a mystery, but I didn't have to wait long for an explanation.

The next morning I had Brownie, Buddy and Blaze pulling on their leashes and instead of Marcus, his mother was sitting on the steps. I warned her, "Puppies with a bladder issue coming through!" She smiled and got up to open the door.

"May I walk with you?" she asked politely. I was happy for the company and said, "Sure!"

She got to the point quickly. "I should have introduced myself. My name is Patti. I believe you met my boy, Marcus, yesterday. I hope he was polite and respectful."

I reassured her he was and commented that he too opened the door for me as she had a moment ago.

"Oh, good, I'm glad. May I share something with you about Marcus?" She seemed anxious to share something so I nodded yes and it didn't take her long to get to the point.

"Marcus had a car accident a few years ago when he was a senior in high school. He was riding with three of his buddies in his best friend's car and a drunk driver hit them. The drunk driver and Marcus' three friends died. Marcus was the only survivor." Patti looked at me to gauge my reaction. I was horrified.

"I am so sorry, Patti. That had to be horrible. It probably still is, huh?" I didn't know what else to say.

"Yes, it was horrible, but worse than the accident is what it did to my boy. He suffered a severe brain injury which affected his short term memory. The doctor said that he probably will never regain his ability to retain new information, other than that from before the accident. It really limits his ability to work or to relate to strangers. Did you notice anything strange when you talked to him?" Patti asked with hope in her voice that I didn't notice anything.

I didn't want to lie but at the same time I wanted to reassure Patti. "You know everyone acts a little off in the early morning. The important thing to me was he was very cordial. Believe it or not, not everyone treats thirteen-year-olds with any kind of regard whatsoever. Your son treated me with kindness. And I appreciated it."

Patti seemed to be happy with that and I was glad to have an explanation for Marcus' strange behavior. Before we knew it, we had returned to the front door and wished each other a good morning. The three dogs wagged a goodbye and Patti gave them each a pat. Before she left she said, "Thank you for letting me walk with you. I enjoyed walking with the dogs. Both Marcus and I love animals."

"Anytime," I said, never dreaming where that simple one-word response may lead. I had no time to think about it now. Houdini was eagerly awaiting his walk.

Sunday was over quickly. After taking care of several cats and walking several dogs, I was glad when Bob arrived to take Houdini home. Anita called to confirm she was home from her conference and thanked me for taking such good care of her babies. I saw lights on in the cat mama's houses and assumed they were home as well. Time to start reading about the Winnebago native Americans, after a short nap.

What's that noise? I looked at my pink alarm clock and realized it was Monday morning at 5:30 a.m. And another week begins.

CHAPTER 24

Thank God For Thanksgiving

The Monday of the week before Thanksgiving Ms. Hart announced that Thursday would be "practice Thanksgiving." She said that she had ordered a catered Thanksgiving meal that day that the class would eat outside if the day was warm, but inside the cafeteria if the weather didn't cooperate. And Friday would be our Native American presentations with a special arts project. She also told the class that the rest of the week would be devoted to our normal studies.

"And," Ms. Hart's voice took on a different tone. "I highly suggest that next week while you are off school you spend some time reviewing your notes and text books from the beginning of the semester until now. When you come back on Monday, December 1st, we will be doing daily reviews of every subject. Don't worry about anything you learned during our Friday presentations. Only our main subjects will be covered on our semester test on Friday, December 5th."

The class groaned in unison. Even though throughout the semester we had random pop up quizzes and some routine short tests, they weren't a full day test. I already dreaded Friday, December 5th. As soon as I got home my Hello Kitty calendar would be adorned with a sad face and a panic face and a tongue-out ugly face on December 5th.

Monday, Tuesday, Wednesday and Thursday morning passed quickly. We saw the catering truck pull up at 10:00 o'clock and unload outside. The weather was beautiful. It was sixty degrees outside, with no wind, and lots of bright sunshine. As a special treat,

Ms. Hart skipped math class that morning so that we could gather outside to eat an early lunch outside – just like the pilgrims and their Native American guests on Thanksgiving!

The caterers, Spring Forest, were friends of Ms. Hart's and were from the southwest suburbs of Chicago, near Palos Heights, where I grew up. They brought turkey and stuffing (of course), corn, sweet potatoes, green bean casserole, and pumpkin pie for dessert. Jerry had set up tables and chairs outside complete with plastic table covers. And even the paper plates we used were decorated with a turkey theme. The food was good. I was ready for a nap. But Ms. Hart and Jerry had other plans.

After lunch, Jerry blew a whistle and told us to line up in the field next to our makeshift picnic area. He had spray painted two colored stripes on the grass indicating a start and a finish line. Each team of five were to line up in parallel lines behind the start line. He handed the first person of each team a small gourd and explained the rules of the game that was played at the first Thanksgiving. When he blew the whistle, the teams would start to run. While running the first person of the team would hand the gourd to the next person backward over his head. The second person would transfer the gourd to the next person through his legs, and this would continue until one of the teams reached the finish line, winning the game.

We lined up. I joined Steve's team and took the last position hoping the gourd would never make it back to me. The whistle blew and one team blew the rest of us out of the water. It was the boys who played football on the weekend for the community league. At least it wasn't Suzy's team, which was made up of all girls.

I noticed cars pulling up to the curb outside of the school, including my dad in Redbird, the convertible. Because the weather was so nice, he had the top down. Jerry must have noticed too because he blew the whistle and wished everyone a good night. Class dismissed!

I skipped dinner that night and cleaned my room in anticipation of Houdini's arrival the next night. I also started my Native American tribe assignment. (Shhhh…. Don't tell my parents I waited so long!). I really didn't think it would be too difficult. We only had to do a ten minute presentation, after all. I found my envelope and opened it for the first time. It read: OJIBWE. Wait a minute! The outside said Winnebago. Ms. Hart had tricked us. She anticipated that some of us would pick a tribe with which we were familiar. Oh well, Ojibwe Tribe it is!

I did my research on the Ojibwe Tribe and was intrigued that they were the tribe memorialized in Longfellow's poem "The Song of Hiawatha", written in 1855. I looked up the poem and thought to myself, why re-create the words of Longfellow when he did such a good job?

The next day when it was my turn to present the Ojibwe Tribe presentation, I read the poem "The Song of Hiawatha" instead:

By the shore of Gitche Gumee,
By the shining Big-Sea-Water,
At the doorway of his wigwam,
In the pleasant Summer morning,
Hiawatha stood and waited.
All the air was full of freshness,
All the earth was bright and joyous,
And before him, through the sunshine,
Westward toward the neighboring forest
Passed in golden swarms the Ahmo,
Passed the bees, the honey-makers,
Burning, singing in the sunshine.

Bright above him shone the heavens,
Level spread the lake before him;
From its bosom leaped the sturgeon,
Sparkling, flashing in the sunshine;
On its margin the great forest
Stood reflected in the water,
Every tree-top had its shadow,
Motionless beneath the water.

From the brow of Hiawatha

> Gone was every trace of sorrow,
> As the fog from off the water,
> As the mist from off the meadow.
> With a smile of joy and triumph,
> With a look of exultation,
> As of one who in a vision
> Sees what is to be, but is not,
> Stood and waited Hiawatha.

I had hardly begun when Ms. Hart suddenly said, "Stop. Libby, I'd like to see you outside in the hall, please." I looked at Ms. Hart expecting praise but instead she looked…. Angry? Perturbed? She was definitely not happy.

I joined her in the hall. She looked at me and said, "Is your name Longfellow?"

"Ummm…. No?" I answered quietly.

"Well, here's the deal, Libby." I didn't like the way she said Libby.

"Longfellow gets an "A". You get a "D". Be happy I didn't fail you. You did not complete the assignment. I am disappointed in you."

I didn't wait for her to say anything more. I ran down the hall to Henry. He must have sensed my mood because he crawled into my arms just in time to be showered with tears. Moments later Jerry walked in and sat down on the opposite side of the desk. He pushed a piece of leftover pumpkin pie in my direction and Henry looked at me as if to say, "Can I share?"

I muttered, "Thank you," to Jerry and then decided to have just a bite, which led to several bites. Henry got his share and at some point the tears stopped. Jerry had left in the meantime and I saw he had left a note behind. It read, "Some days are better than others. Always try to start and end each day on a happy note. And remember, things could always be worse. Go back to class and hold your head up high, Hiawatha!"

That made me laugh. I dried off my tears and swiped my face in Henry's fur. I put some food in his dish and went back to class with gray fur affixed to my face and the feather in my head that Jerry had left. In an hour it was time to go home and I made it to the end without crying. It helped that I didn't make eye contact with anyone, including Ms. Hart or Steve. I noticed on the board that Ms. Hart had written: DON'T FORGET TO STUDY FOR THE DECEMBER 5TH TEST!

In the remaining hour, after the tribe presentations, Ms. Hart handed out our art project. She gave each of us a dream catcher kit. Mine had pink feathers and beads. Knowing pink was my favorite color, she couldn't be too mad at me.

Right before the bell rang signifying the end of the day, I bagged up my books in my backpack and made a beeline for the door. Steve was right behind me. He took the heavy backpack from me and said, "May I?" as he put the backpack on his shoulders.

"Thanks," I uttered and managed a small smile.

"I like the feather," Steve said as he brushed gray fur from my cheeks. It wasn't the biggest compliment he ever gave me, but at that moment it was the best.

I took the feather from my hair and put it in his. "It's yours." He smiled as he took my hand and led me to my dad's car.

I dropped his hand right before reaching the car. I know my dad saw us holding hands, but to his credit, he didn't say anything. Instead, he asked Steve if he would be at birdwatching the next day.

"Sure am!" Steve exclaimed. "Are you?" he asked my dad.

"Sure am. And so is Libby. It's about time she's introduced to the world of birdwatching, don't you think?" my dad asked Steve.

"I can't wait. See you both tomorrow!" Steve seemed happy at the prospect.

"Tootles Steve." I turned to get in the car and then remembered he had my backpack.

"I need my backpack please," I said to Steve. But my dad was already retrieving the heavy backpack from Steve and put it in the backseat of the car.

I waved to Steve as my dad raced out of the parking spot. I looked over at my dad. What was that expression on his face? Oh, no! It was the dad version of the mom smirk!

'Don't worry,' he said. "Your secret is safe with me." I added another Thanksgiving blessing for his understanding to my list.

CHAPTER 25

Thanksgiving Week Begins

Miraculously the only pet obligation I had the Saturday and Sunday before Thanksgiving was Houdini. My mom volunteered to stay with Houdini while I went birdwatching with my dad. Also miraculous was the fact that she didn't chide me about Steve. In fact, she didn't even mention him. Another Thanksgiving blessing!

Birdwatching was… interesting. The most impressive thing wasn't the birds. It was the enthusiasm of the bird watchers group. Everyone was so friendly and willing to help teach me about the birds we saw. And at the end of the couple of hours event they declared me their lucky charm because they encountered more birds than usual that day. I have to admit it was more fun than I thought. Looking through the binoculars gave me a new perspective of how beautiful birds can be. And watching them interact and feed, especially the water fowl, was fascinating too.

My dad had prearranged with Steve's parents to take him out for lunch afterwards. I wondered where dad had in mind. Maybe Gibson's? Maybe Manny's? Maybe Mr. Gyros? We drove through Chinatown but we had never eaten in Chinatown before. We always had carry-out. And then a few blocks east of Chinatown we pulled into the parking lot of a familiar white building. "WHITE CASTLE!" I screamed. "We're going to WHITE CASTLE!" I looked over at Steve expecting to see excitement, but instead he looked confused.

"What, you don't like White Castle?" I asked.

"I've never had White Castle," he said. "I don't know what to expect."

"You can expect the highest form of culinary delight in the world," I said as I pictured my personal sack of three white castle slider cheeseburgers. "Don't worry, I'll help you order."

We sat in the small booth with stacks of small square containers of White Castle burgers in front of us. And fries. And chicken rings. And onion rings. No one talked. We just ate. And at the end Steve's comment was, "I doubt Thanksgiving will come anywhere near how delicious this meal was. Can I get some to go to share with my folks?"

My dad laughed and ordered some to go for us as well. I assumed they were for mom's lunch, but when we got home, dad said to mom, "Here you are. As ordered. 10 white castle hamburgers – no pickle."

My mom took the bag and put it in the refrigerator. "Aren't you gonna eat them while they're hot?" I asked.

"Don't be silly. She answered. They're my secret ingredient for Thanksgiving stuffing." Now I understood what made mom's stuffing so yummy. I started an internal countdown to Thanksgiving.

"Hey, mom, where's Houdini?" I asked.

"Who Houdini," she said teasing while motioning to the back patio.

I hurried outside to the patio to make sure he was okay and sure enough, there he was basking in the sun. He got up wagging and jumped in my lap as I took a seat, also in the sun. He was a little big for my lap but he served as a good blanket. The next thing I knew, we were being called inside for dinner. We were given strict instructions by Bob that Houdini could not have table food, but we did move his doggy dishes to under the table so he could eat at the same time. He made a few attempts at begging for table food but eventually gave up and gobbled up his dog food. After dinner Houdini ran to the end of my bed and whimpered. I lifted him up and he quickly settled in for a post-dinner nap. He truly led a dog's life.

The next day I decided to get a head start on my studying for the December 5th test. I opened my backpack and a note fell out. It was in Ms. Hart's handwriting. It read: "Dear Libby, I am sorry about the misunderstanding regarding the Native American tribe assignment. Please feel free to write a short report on whatever tribe you choose and we'll get rid of that "D". Have a lovely Thanksgiving. Ms. Hart". I guess that was fair. Maybe I would pick the Winnebago tribe now, given the choice. I don't think Longfellow wrote a poem about them.

The rest of the day was spent writing my Winnebago report, and reading notes from my geography, history and English classes. I skipped math, for today. Bob came right on schedule, and Houdini was slow to leave. I think he was getting used to getting a lot of attention from me, my mom and dad.

On Monday I had my usual pet sitting schedule, with the exception of Hans, whose mother took the week off, and a later walking time for Anita's dogs. She asked that since I was off from school if I could take them out on Monday through Wednesday at 8 a.m. instead of 6 a.m. I was very happy to accommodate her. Even the dogs seemed happier to go out later. On Monday morning I was surprised to see Patti and Marcus in the entryway. Before I could say "Good Morning" Marcus said, "Oh, you walk dogs, don't you?" I remembered what his mom had said about his short term memory.

"Yes, I do. Since you and your mom are all dressed to go outside, would you like to take a walk with the four of us?" I motioned to the dogs.

Marcus turned to his mother. "Can we Ma?" His mother was quick to say yes and opened the door. We took longer than I usually do and at one point I asked Marcus if he'd like to "take the reins." His mother warned him to take a quick grip and the dogs seemed to sense that they should behave. All the same, I sighed a breath of relief when we all returned safely to inside the building. Patti thanked me for letting them walk with me and Marcus asked if we could go again. Like now.

"Not now, but maybe another day," I said non-committedly. Patti mouthed thank you and we parted ways. I returned the dogs to Anita's apartment and was surprised to see her up and dressed.

"Libby, how was your walk this morning?" She asked as if she already knew the answer. And then I saw the drapes were open. I wondered if she saw Marcus walking the dogs. I decided it was best to be up front about allowing Marcus to walk the dogs.

"The dogs were thrilled this morning because they had the company of two of our newest neighbors – Patti and her son Marcus. They love dogs, especially yours, and asked if they could accompany us on our walk. In fact, Marcus took the leashes from me for a short minute so I could blow my nose." I figured a little white lie wasn't too out of line if it made Anita not fire me for allowing someone else access to her fur babies.

"I did see that and I was thrilled," Anita said.

"Huh?" I said, at a loss for words. *Why would she be thrilled?*

"I so enjoyed getting two extra hours of sleep this morning and I thought if only Libby could let me sleep those two extra hours every day. And then I saw that tall boy handling Blaze, Brownie and Buddy so competently and the thought came to me! Maybe Libby would hire him to walk my dogs in the morning!" Anita looked at me expectantly.

My heart dropped. That was a lot of money to lose and these were my first dog clients. What if the other pet clients decided to switch as well? Heck, Mimi already fired me.

Anita must have sensed my hesitation and said, "Well it's something to think about. Maybe the boy wouldn't want to do it and I'd have to meet him first."

I made an instant decision. "Anita, of course you should meet him, but you'd need to meet with his mother first and she'll explain the circumstances. The one thing I'd ask is that you allow me to walk the dogs when my school schedule doesn't conflict, and that officially I'd keep you on as a client and Marcus (that's his name) would work for me."

Anita was quick to say, "Of course. Do you have his mother's number?"

"How about tomorrow I'll have her come with me after the walk and she can talk with you then?"

"Perfect!" Anita said. And as I headed for the door she said, "You know Libby – you will still be our favorite pet nanny, don't you?" I smiled but inside felt sad.

I felt even sadder when I got home and had to face math homework. I avoided it for a short while when I took care of the herd of cats – Charley, Felix and Odin, and for the first time, Chloe. Her mother, Cecelia, left her key with George. She had an emergency at work and needed to start very early, before she had a chance to take care of Chloe. I kicked myself for not making an appointment with Cecelia to get a tour of her cat's surroundings and where her food was kept.

I found George after I took care of the first three cats and he offered to go with me to Chloe's apartment. As he unlocked the door, a splash of white escaped out the door and down the hall. George went running and I stood guard at the door in case the cat came back. George came back a minute later followed by Marcus carrying a struggling cat.

"Hi, my name is Marcus. Who are you?" he asked politely.

George said, "This is Libby. She's here to take care of Chloe, the cat."

"Oh, I can do that. Is this Chloe's house?" Marcus asked as he went inside the apartment. Instinctively Marcus went to the cupboard and took out Chloe's food and then stooped to clean out Chloe's litterbox while Chloe rubbed up against him and purred before eating her food. Afterward, Marcus refilled her water bowl and took out some cat treats from a container on the counter. At least I hoped they were cat treats as they were unlabeled.

"Marcus, do you have a cat?" George asked.

"Not that I can remember, but I sure do wish I had one. I'd take real good care of it. Well, I better get home before my mom worries about me." Marcus left and Chloe started to run after him.

"Oh, no you don't Chloe!" George grabbed her before she could escape a second time.

"I guess our work is done here. What do you think, Libby?" George asked.

"I think I need to hire Marcus. I'm going to talk to his mother." George nodded in agreement and somehow I knew that he had determined that long before I came up with the idea.

The next morning, I talked with Patti about hiring Marcus for my overflow. She agreed that at least for the immediate future, both she and Marcus would handle pet sitting chores together. We visited Anita after walking her dogs, and I dropped Chloe a note and put

it under her door. I advised both Pet Nanny customers that I was expanding my business by adding additional staff.

I wouldn't miss my 6 a.m. dog walking duties, but I would miss Brownie, Buddy and Blaze.

Thanksgiving dawned early and cold. I was glad that I didn't have to walk any dogs today. I still had to take care of cats because their mothers were visiting relatives for Thanksgiving meals. I checked with Chloe's mother, and she said that she and her cat were serving an intimate Thanksgiving for two. I assume she meant her and the cat, but you never know.

What was that smell? It smelled like... WHITE CASTLES! I bounded out of bed and hurried into the kitchen. "Mom, are we having White Castles for breakfast?"

"Well, as a matter of fact, I sent your dad to White Castle this morning to buy more for stuffing because somehow the ones in the refrigerator disappeared. I thought he might as well get some more for breakfast. Help yourself!" My mom knew the way to my stomach. Best Thanksgiving breakfast ever!

I asked my mom, half-heartedly because I don't like to cook, if I could help and she was quick to say, "No. I don't want to have the firemen over for the holiday." I took the cue and returned to my studies, including finalizing my Winnebago Tribe essay. I even studied some math problems and surprised myself that I was able to do them effortlessly. I heard the bell ring and knew it had to be Aunt Lori. I finished up one more history chapter and then when into the kitchen.

"Hi, Aunt Lori" was on my lips but I stopped when I saw Aunt Lori rubbing my mother's tummy. Why would she be doing that? Just as I had that thought my Aunt Lori turned and greeted me warmly. "Hi Pumpkin! You ready for some good gobbles?"

I was still fixated with her hand on my mom's stomach, but I couldn't think of a polite way to ask why she was doing that. Instead I said, "Happy gobbles. I sure am. In fact, is the turkey in the oven, mom?"

My Aunt Lori answered instead of my mom. "I just checked it out! Yes, there is a turkey in the oven and the bun is in there too!" Both my mom and Aunt Lori laughed hysterically. At what, I have no idea. Grown-ups are so strange sometimes.

But before I could think about it too much the door bell rang. My mom said, "Well don't just stand there. Answer the door. It's probably one of your clients."

I quickly went to the door and was faced with a panicky looking Jerry holding Henry who jumped from his arms into mine. "Libby, can you take care of Henry today? I was invited to George's house for Thanksgiving and his wife said Henry is not invited. I don't want to leave him alone all day and I don't know how long I'll be away. I promise to pick him up no later than 9 p.m. tonight. Is it okay?"

I didn't answer right away because I was so happy to see Henry. And then I sensed a dark presence behind me. Yep, it was my mother.

"Hey, mom. Can we help Jerry MY SCHOOL VICE PRINCIPAL out and watch Henry today? I promise he won't eat much." Meanwhile Jerry made his way to the kitchen.

"Hey are you making the White Castle stuffing recipe? I wish George's wife was making that stuffing. Do you need a tester?" And without waiting for a response Jerry dipped a wooden spoon in the pot and smacked his lips. And then he noticed Aunt Lori sitting at the kitchen table.

"Perfection," he proclaimed while still staring at Aunt Lori. I wasn't sure if he meant the stuffing or Aunt Lori.

"Henry can stay on one condition: that you mind him and don't let him get out. And if he does, Jerry, you won't hold us liable." My mom looked at both me and Jerry waiting for our agreement and we both nodded yes. Then she looked at Henry, and said, "Do you agree not to be a pain-in-the-neck?" Henry meowed amicably and my mom reluctantly said, "Okay, Henry can stay."

Jerry turned to leave and said to Aunt Lori, "Will you be here when I get back?"

"I sure will and I'll save you some of that stuffing you like so much," Aunt Lori promised.

"Great! Great! See you later then." Jerry stumbled backwards to the door unwilling to stop looking at Aunt Lori. You'd think he'd be more worried about leaving Henry. Grownups!

Mom rang the dinner bell (actually the alarm on the microwave) to announce dinner was served and Henry followed us to the dinner

table and took a place at an empty chair. My mom reluctantly put a small saucer on the table with milk and Henry politely licked it up as we ate and sneaked small turkey tidbits to him under the table. Dinner was delicious. Everyone agreed mom was hired to make Christmas dinner too.

Henry acted like he lived with us forever. He made his napping corner in Houdini's bed. He ate out of Houdini's dishes which my mother filled with turkey scraps, unaware that we had fed him at the table. He even drank from Houdini's water dish. After dinner he jumped from human lap to lap and sensed not to overstay his welcome on my mom's lap.

Everyone took up places in the living room to watch some Thanksgiving Hallmark movie my mom insisted on watching when someone knocked VERY loudly at the door. Henry cowered between the corner of the couch and my lap as my dad answered the door.

We heard him ask, "Can I help you?" And then I heard the shrill voice of Mimi, mother of Einstein.

"I want my cat back. I heard a meow in here. I know you catnapped Einstein. Hand him over."

Without an invitation, Mimi came in the door and into the living room. Henry hid under the blanket on the couch and thankfully didn't make a sound. Mimi looked frantically around the room and screamed, "There he is. My poor little Einstein. How dare you throw him outside!"

We all looked in the direction of her gaze, and there was Einstein on the patio, perched on the windowsill, looking in the window. My mom went to the patio door and scooped up Einstein who happily snuggled in her arms. I looked at Einstein and wanted to scream, "What have you done with him?" to Mimi. He had lost weight and his eyes were tearing and some of his fur had disappeared. Einstein spotted me on the couch and sprang onto the back of the couch. At the same time Houdini popped out to see what all the fuss was about and came face-to-face with Einstein. There was a long moment before either cat reacted and then they both snuggled on my lap, far away from Mimi's clutches.

My dad addressed Mimi. "Happy Thanksgiving, Mimi. I can honestly tell you that no one in this family has seen Einstein since you fired my daughter. And that's not from lack of wanting to see him. He was Libby's favorite cat, at least until Henry here entered the picture. I can tell you that it doesn't take a cat expert to see your cat is not doing very well. I would guess that he escaped your apartment, came into the courtyard, and climbed the fence to our patio. I don't know if he smelled Libby or just knew where she lived, but he was definitely looking for her. But understand this: there was no catnapping."

Mimi looked mildly embarrassed but wouldn't back down completely. "I wouldn't be surprised if she lured him here."

I finally felt the need to defend myself. "I was fired and I have honored your wishes that I not see Einstein again, but I wish that I hadn't seen him in this shape. Did your new cat sitter do this to him?" I asked.

Mimi said, "There is no cat sitter. I figure he could fend for himself. But, this is hard for me to admit, I think he needs you to return as his pet nanny. Would you be willing?"

Patience, I pleaded with myself. Don't act too excited. Put the pom poms away. "I would need a raise", I said, holding my breath that I didn't ruin my chances of a life with Einstein again.

"That's fair," said Mimi. "It's a deal," said Mimi.

"One more thing," I said. "Ditch the kitty cam. Einstein and I need our privacy."

"Consider it gone!" Mimi said as she took a reluctant Einstein from me. Henry meowed a sad goodbye to his new friend.

"I'll email you my schedule for next week and slip a key under your door." At the sound of the door clicking my mom and dad high fived and a confused Aunt Lori got another glass of wine to celebrate. I turned to Henry and said, "Don't worry. Einstein might have been here before you, but you're my forever kitty." And I wondered why I said that, because in truth he was Jerry's kitty. But for the moment, I was speaking the truth. He was my kitty for the day.

CHAPTER 26

December

As promised, Ms. Hart started the first day back from Thanksgiving vacation with an intense review of our studies in all subjects for the first four days of the week. On Friday we all nervously anticipated our all-day test. Ms. Hart announced that morning that before the test we needed to be prepared for the rigorous task ahead of us so she handed out what she called "brain food", otherwise known as chocolate donuts.

At 7:30 a.m. we were told to put the donuts down and pick up our pencils. Ms. Hart handed out the tests print-side down. She said this was part 1 of the test which would cover Math. We had 50 minutes to finish it. She counted down from 5, 4, 3, 2, 1, and instructed us to TURN THE TEST OVER AND START. At the end of the 50 minutes she blew a whistle indicating that we should stop.

We had a ten minute break in between test parts and had 50 minutes to finish each section. I was surprised that I finished the Math section in less time than required, but other subjects took me to the time limit to finish. We all finished before our quitting time at noon and this time Ms. Hart fed us juice boxes and Goldfish crackers before we left. I'm not sure what the significance of the snack was, but I gobbled it up nonetheless.

I thanked Ms. Hart for the treats as we all shuffled out the door, tired from taking our test. Ms. Hart asked me to stay behind for a moment and I really wanted to run. Everyone stepped up their pace seeing that someone was asked to stay after class, and not wanting to be asked to do the same.

"Is something wrong, Ms. Hart?" I asked, afraid of the answer.

"No, not at all. I just wanted to assure you that since you didn't have a long enough break to take care of Henry, I did it when you all were busy taking the geography section." Ms. Hart reported.

"Oh, no! Thank you so much. I completely forgot about Henry," I confessed. And I had this sudden guilty feeling that I may have forgotten something else important.

"Have a good weekend, Libby. Don't worry so much. By the way, your Native American Tribe assignment was very good. You got an "A", *Hiawatha*," she said kiddingly. I guess it would take a while before I lived down what I called the Longfellow Booboo.

My dad was waiting at the curb with Steve. "Is everything okay?" they both asked in unison.

"Sure is," I said. "Just some teacher-student confidential matter that needed to be addressed."

Both my dad and Steve shrugged their shoulders and asked if I'd be joining them for birdwatching on Saturday morning. I begged off saying I needed to review my Pet Nanny Calendar. I said it as a reprieve to get out of bird watching but it ended up that looking at the Pet Nanny Calendar for the weekend was imperative.

As soon as I got home I looked at the calendar and all I could see was ink. Everyone was making up for being homebound for the holiday last weekend and leaving this weekend. Before I could study the calendar further the doorbell rang. I answered the door on the third ring and Mimi stood on the other side of the door.

"I am on my way out. Here's my key. Please check on Einstein at least twice a day starting at dinner time. I'll be back on Monday about this time so please check on Einstein before you leave for school." Without waiting for a reply, Mimi left me standing in the doorway. I looked at the calendar in my hand and noticed Einstein was not on my list but almost ever other client was.

My dad called from the kitchen. "Who was that at the door?" I whistled the Wicked Witch theme from the Wizard of Oz.

He answered, "Oh Mimi. Let me guess – you're on duty this weekend."

"Yep. For Einstein and many, many others," I said, already tired from the effort of being the Pet Nanny.

My mom came home shortly after with sushi from the French Market in the Ogilvie Train Station. It lightened my mood for a moment until I looked at the calendar again and groaned.

After lunch I took Marcus' first commission for taking care of Anita's dogs and Cecelia's cat. He answered on the first knock, and looked at me without recognition. "Hi, Marcus. Is your mom home?"

Before I finished my sentence Patti came to the door. "I'll take care of Libby, Marcus. You can go back to your program." Marcus smiled and disappeared.

"I brought Marcus' pay for the week. I sure am thankful you were both able and willing to help," I said handing over the week's pay.

Patti said, "You have no idea how happy it made Marcus every morning when I asked him if he'd like to take care of some animals today. And I also enjoyed getting out to walk. Thank you for "hiring" us. Are we on for next week – same schedule?

"For sure! But I wonder if you'd be willing to give up some of your time this weekend as well? I went through my calendar, and it would be great if you and Marcus could help this weekend," I said, hoping she'd be agreeable.

"Just let us know when and where, and we're there!" she said agreeably.

"That's great, Patti. I am going to go home now and make the schedule and will be back with whatever keys you need. You still have Anita's and Cecelia's, right?" I asked.

"Yes we do. And we put them in a safe place right here." She opened a cabinet door, and I saw keys suspended from hooks. Above the hooks were stickers with the initials "A" and "C" for Anita and Cecelia. *Wow!* I thought. *It took me months to figure out a system for my client's keys and Patti had it down the first week!*

"Well, thanks. I'll stop by before dinner. May I bring Hans with me? I take him out for a walk at 6 p.m." I hoped she'd say yes.

"I tell you what. How about we all take Hans for a walk? It's getting dark now that it's December. That way we'd have safety in numbers," Patti suggested.

"OK. See you later, gator." I was surprised that I never thought about that, but Patti was right. That night I felt much more confident.

CHAPTER 27

Christmas Comes This Time Of Year

On Sunday night when Bob picked up Houdini he noticed that Houdini seemed tired. I explained that he now had three dogwalkers and every one of us liked to take him for walks over the weekend. He laughed and said we should change his name to Marathon Dog. Houdini wagged at the attention and was slow to leave. I was glad that he seemed as happy to stay with us as we were to have him over each weekend.

Einstein and I picked up right where we left off, but before I started sharing my stories with Einstein, I searched high and low for Mimi's pet cam. I split the schedule for the other cats with Marcus and each day I double checked the calendar to make sure each pet was covered. After Houdini left I realized Houdini wasn't the only tired puppy – so was I.

"Whatcha up to?" my mom asked.

"I have a project I want to start for Friday's presentation," I answered, praying she wouldn't offer to help.

"What kind of project?" my mom asked. Here it comes.... "Maybe I can help?"

And before I could let her down gently, my dad suggested that he could help too.

"Well, I don't know that I can explain it very well. Maybe I should just muddle through it myself," I said.

"Don't be silly, honey. We're here for you. What is the project?"

They both looked so excited to help, I couldn't say no. I explained the project, due this Friday, was to pick an ethnicity and make a short presentation on how that group celebrates Christmas (or a like holiday in December) and to bring a treat to share that is part of that celebration.

"Oh," they said unenthusiastically in unison. "You've got this!" my mom said.

"Let me know when you get to the treat part. I can be a taster," my dad said.

And just when I was thinking it might be fun to do this as a family, both of my parents decided not to help. It was getting close to St. Lucia Day so I decided to pick "Swedish" as my ethnicity. I made Swedish meatballs from my great grandma's recipe, which was to buy refrigerated meatballs and serve them in a creamy gravy, sprinkled with dill. My mom let me borrow the crock pot to keep them warm and put a box of Swedish pepperkaker (ginger) cookies in my backpack to share with the class. But the crowning touch was my wreath with small electric candles taped to the wreath that I wore on my head, just like St. Lucia.

On Friday we had an all-day feast at school interspersed with presentations on what our selected ethnic group did to celebrate the holiday. I explained that St. Lucia Day was celebrated in Sweden on December 13th. A girl was selected to play St. Lucia, who wore a white dress with a red sash and wore a crown just like mine. And with that I flipped a switch which should have made my candles glow, but evidently the battery was dead. I didn't miss a beat. I explained I didn't want to cause a fire hazard by having lit candles. Ironically the candles represent the fire that burned St. Lucia in real life centuries ago. My speech wasn't a hit but the meatballs and ginger cookies were.

When class was over that day the place was a mess. I asked Ms. Hart if she wanted help cleaning up, and she said, no. That was okay. She had no where to be and all day to get there. I never thought about what Ms. Hart did outside of school. "Are you sure?" I asked.

"Absolutely," she answered and said "Go on. Get! Your dad is waiting."

On the way home I said to my dad, "I don't think Ms. Hart has anywhere to go for Christmas."

"That's a shame. Did Steve tell you bird watching is canceled tomorrow. Do you want to help me go Christmas shopping tomorrow?" It's like my dad hadn't heard a thing I said.

I would try again. "Hey, dad. Do you think we could invite Ms. Hart to dinner on Christmas?"

"What did you say Libby?" My dad was so distracted today.

"Never mind. I'll ask mom," I said, not expecting an answer.

"Hey, you know I could really use your help Christmas shopping for your mother. I think she needs some new clothes." My dad looked at me waiting for my answer.

"Sure, dad. I'll ask Patti and Marcus to watch Houdini while we're out," I said.

Whose bright idea was it to shop mid-December for Christmas? I asked myself. The mall, an hour away from downtown, was jammed. We parked at the outer edge of the parking lot and were lucky to get that spot. My dad marched into Macy's Department Store and consulted the directory. He said, "You don't believe in Santa anymore, do you?"

"Umm. No. Not since like first grade." I said, a little upset that he didn't know that already.

"Great. Then, can I ask you to pick out some outfits from Santa while I look for your mom in this next department?" I looked to see where he pointed, and there was a big "M" sign suspended from the ceiling. *Wow*, I thought. *Who knew there was a special section for "MOM'S"?*

"Sure, dad. You look for mom clothes in the Mom Section and I'll go over here to juniors." I didn't notice the confused look on his face, but as we parted ways, we agreed to meet back at this point in about an hour.

One hour later we met at the designated spot and my dad had at least ten shopping bags in his hands. "Where's your stuff, Libby?" he asked in a panic.

"My stuff is on hold at the counter over there. I told the lady I didn't have a credit card and that you were shopping for my mom in the "M" department. She told me she'd hold it until I found you."

"Well, let's go buy your Santa gifts! I hope you got some things you like," my dad said as he swiped his credit card and tried to carry four more bags of clothes.

When we returned home mom was on the floor of the living room surrounded by boxes of ornaments and trimmings. She had managed to put up the artificial Christmas tree with the help of Marcus and Patti who had come over for their weekly pay. My mom asked my dad for help to get up and as I glanced over I noticed she had gained even more weight. She actually looked plump. I wondered if my dad took that into account when he bought her new clothes.

My mom was speaking to me, but I missed what she had said. She hated when I didn't focus. "Sorry, mom. What did you say?"

"Marcus and Patti said they had no Christmas plans. How do you two feel about having them over for Christmas dinner?" Both my dad and I said, "Sure," together and I took the opportunity to further expand our Christmas guest list.

"You know who else has nothing to do on Christmas? My teacher, Ms. Hart. Can we invite her too?" I asked. Both my mom and dad said "Sure."

"Well as long as we are on the subject," my dad said, "I overheard Jerry talking with George and it sounded like George's wife is going out of town to be with her side of the family and George is staying behind to work. What do you think about inviting Jerry and George too?" While my mom and I both agreed I was wondering if there was enough room to seat them all.

After dinner, my mom got on the phone and invited Ms. Hart and Patti and Marcus. They all gladly accepted. I opened the door, knowing George would be there, and asked if he'd like to come to Christmas dinner with Jerry. And George said, "We thought you'd never ask! Hey, those Christmas decorations aren't gonna hang themselves!" And without hesitation he came in and started decorating the tree, with our help.

At school the next Monday – the last week before Christmas and New Year's break – I asked Steve what he and his family were doing for Christmas. He said, "I'm not sure. We had a plumbing leak this weekend and my mom said she was in no mood to celebrate."

"Would you all like to come to our house for Christmas dinner?" I asked. Steve couldn't wait to ask his parents, who readily agreed to join us. I was thinking, maybe if we all didn't fit, the kid's table could be on the patio!

Finally, Christmas was here, and as was tradition, when everyone was up, we opened gifts. We rolled dice to determine who would be first, second and third to open gifts. My dad got high score making him the first to unwrap. My mom was second. And I was last. But that was okay. I KNEW I was finally getting my puppy or kitten. I overheard my parents the night before, on Christmas Eve, saying that they were sure Libby would love the family's new addition.

My dad opened his annual gift of pajamas, new work shirts, ties, and a magazine subscription to Birds and Blooms.

My mom opened her pile of boxes containing "mom" clothes. And as she opened the first one I told her that when dad and I shopped at Macy's I never noticed that the store had a Mom's department. My mom looked at my dad and said what is she talking about? My dad sheepishly pointed to a tag on one of the clothes, and my mom and they both burst out laughing.

I was confused but wished my mom would hurry up. I was anxious to open my gifts. But first I admired the clothes my dad selected for my mom. They were all colorful and even looked to be the right size - LARGE! Good job, Dad!

Finally, it was my turn. I ripped open the first box and it was a new winter coat and gloves stuffed into the pockets. I surveyed the other boxes looking for something that could contain a dog or a cat. Maybe some of those boxes might, if it was a small dog or cat. Then I opened a second box that ended up being new boots. They were nice, but they weren't a dog or a cat. The next box rattled too much to be a dog or a cat, but I was thrilled at the new books it held. The final box was definitely clothes. My mom and dad looked anxious

as I opened it. It was a sweatshirt with writing on it. It said, "I'M A BIG SISTER".

"Mom, I think someone swapped your box. This says "I'm a big sister." I looked at her with disappointment.

"Come on Libby. Don't tell me you didn't notice me throwing up. Or gaining weight. Or your dad shopping in the "M" ("Maternity") department?" My mom looked at me exasperated and a little disappointed.

I looked at the shirt and then at my mother and started to cry. "But when I asked for an addition to the family – I wanted a dog or a cat. Not a baby sister or brother!"

"Libby!" My dad used a voice I rarely heard. He was angry. "Apologize to your mom. This is a happy moment for all of us. And that's right. You DID ask for an addition to the family and that's just what you'll get: a baby brother or sister in the Spring, just like you wished."

I wasn't sure how this happened, but they both looked so desperate for me to join in the joy, I summoned up my best "Yayyyy" and gave them each a hug.

Just then the doorbell rang. Oh no, what did I forget now? I automatically assumed I forgot to take care of one of my pets. But when I opened the door, there was George and Jerry. George carried several bags and Jerry an animal carrier with a bow. Noooooo.... Was it happening? Was I getting a pet of my very own? I could hardly contain my excitement.

And then a familiar meow sounded from the carrier as Jerry handed it over to me.

I opened the carrier and Henry jumped out and climbed up my leg demanding to be held.

"What's happening? I don't understand," I uttered.

Jerry said, "I can't deny Henry a proper home any longer. The school is no place for a cat. I asked your parents if Henry could live with all of you and they said they thought it was probably going to be your favorite gift ever, next to your new baby sister or brother, of course." *Wow. Did everyone know my mother was pregnant?*

I didn't have the heart to tell my parents the cat was my favorite paws down but thanked Jerry profusely while George set up a selection of cat toys for Henry throughout the apartment. Meanwhile Henry fell asleep in my arms somehow knowing he was home.

Later that afternoon everyone took a spot around the long folding table that my parents used for my 13th birthday party. It was decorated beautifully and fit everyone perfectly. Aunt Lori took a place next to Jerry. I sat next to Steve and set a place on my other side with a saucer of milk for Henry. It was a potluck dinner, with my mom making the main course of a Honey Baked Ham. Steve's family brought several side dishes, including a Crave Case of White Castle burgers. There was more food on the table than there was at the school Ethnicity Christmas Feast. My dad stood and made a toast, "To our friends and my beautiful family and its new addition." Everyone raised their glasses and I turned to Henry. "Dad's toasting you, Henry. You're our new addition!" Henry meowed in appreciation and my dad growled.

I saw my dad scowl and figured out he wasn't talking about Henry the cat but instead the new baby. I stood, grabbing my eggnog, and made a toast, "And to my new baby sister or brother!" My mom and dad smiled as they clicked their glasses.

Just then my mom's phone chimed signaling an incoming call. No doubt someone was calling to wish her a merry Christmas. She answered on the second ring after looking at caller ID and said in a cheery voice, "Merry Christmas, Kara, Carl and Rocky! How is everything in Seattle?"

I was thrilled to hear that our old neighbors were calling and especially thrilled at the prospect of "talking" to Rocky, their dog. We hadn't heard from them since their recent move to Seattle, and I missed them terribly – especially Rocky, who was one of my favorite pet nanny charges.

I noticed that my mom's mood had changed drastically from her cheery tone a moment ago. There was a hesitation in her conversation and my mom looked confused. My mom's tone was subdued and soft. She uttered into the phone, "Kara, Kara. Why are you crying? What's wrong, Kara?"

But I knew, even before Kara shared her sad news.

The end.

"Of Note"

The author wishes to recognize the following inspirations included in The Pet Nanny 2.

Turn, Turn, Turn – a song made famous by the group The Yard Birds. Enjoy the music video by The Byrds performing Turn! Turn! Turn! (To Everything There Is A Season), originally released in 1965. All rights reserved by Columbia Records, a division of Sony Music Entertainment.

Of note: the song Turn, Turn, Turn was inspired by the bible verse Ecclesiastes (3:1-8).

The Song of Hiawatha – a poem written in 1855 by Henry Wadsworth Longfellow, inspired by his friendship with the Ojibwe Tribe.

DISCLAIMER:

This is a work of fiction. Names, characters, businesses, places, events, locales and incidents are either the products of the author's imagination or used in a fictitious manner. Any resemblance to actual persons, living or dead, or actual events is purely coincidental, with the notable exception of the two acknowledgements above.

www.ingramcontent.com/pod-product-compliance
Lightning Source LLC
LaVergne TN
LVHW010217070526
838199LV00062B/4636